CHEATING THE FUTURE
FOR THE PAST

BY: CHENELL PARKER

Chapter 1

After successfully grabbing her phone from the night stand, Keller ran into the bathroom just in time before her bedroom door came crashing down. Once she was inside, she hurriedly flung her body on the floor in front of the locked door and prayed that her weight was enough to keep it from being kicked in. Keller's heart plummeted to her stomach when she heard the doorknob being twisted.

"Open this door before I kick this bitch down!" Leo yelled as he continued to tug on the handle.

"Leave me alone!" Keller cried through the blood filled split on her lip.

She hadn't been home for a good five minutes before Leo went into one of his tantrums and backhanded her, busting her lip. They'd been getting along great for weeks, but all of that was for nothing now. He was back to his old ways and she was fed up with it. Being a nail tech and make-up artist sometimes had Keller working longer hours than usual. It always depended on how many clients she had booked in a day. That particular day proved to be a busy one since they had a concert in town. Most of Keller's customers made appointments, but she wasn't opposed to taking walk-ins. If they didn't mind waiting until she took care of her appointments, they got serviced just the same. She'd made a good name for herself around New Orleans and she didn't want to lose business by turning people away. Unfortunately, Leo, her boyfriend of five years didn't understand that. He wanted her to be home at a certain time, but she didn't have a set schedule. He'd called her at least ten times in less than two hours, but her work load didn't allow her to answer for him. He was enraged when she walked through the door and tried to offer up an explanation.

"Bitch open this door! You must be trying to hide and call your other nigga!" Leo yelled in a fit of rage.

Every time Keller didn't answer the phone or was late coming home, he always accused her of cheating. Although he'd done his fair share of dirt, Keller had never cheated on him once. Leo was rumored to have made a baby on her and all, but she still remained faithful. After dialing a number on her phone, Keller waited for someone to pick up.

"Hey girl," Leo's mother Patrice answered.

"You need to come and get your son before I send his ass to jail," Keller cried on the other end.

"Send his ass then. I'm so sick of that boy and his bullshit. What did he do this time?" Patrice asked her.

"He hit me. I was at work and didn't answer when he called and now he's mad," Keller answered.

"So you calling my mama on me now? The fuck you think Pat gon' do?" Leo yelled loud enough for his mother to hear.

"He's so damn stupid, but that's your fault Keller. That's my son and I love him, but I told you to leave his ass a long time ago. You keep letting him charm his way back into your life, but Leo ain't gon' change. He's just like his daddy and can't keep his hands to himself. I told you what I went through and you're going through the same shit. Leave his ass alone and don't take him back. You got too much going for yourself to put up with that. I told you that a man who doesn't respect his own mama will never respect you," Patrice argued.

"I know Pat, but can you at least come here to calm him down until I leave," Keller begged. She hated that she and Leo shared a car. Now she would have to find a ride to get away.

"I see you still ain't tired yet, huh? You just said that you were going to call the police. I know you're not because you don't want him to go to jail. That's how I know you're gonna take him back."

"I just want to get my stuff and get out of here with no problems," Keller replied.

She couldn't deny that there was some truth to what her mother-in-law was saying, but she wasn't trying to hear that at the moment. She just needed to escape Leo's wrath and give him some time to cool off.

"I'm sorry, but I'm not getting out of my bed this time of the night to deal with that. It's almost midnight. Call the police and let them haul his abusive ass right to jail," Patrice replied.

Keller never called her own mama because she knew that Monique didn't play that. She would show up to their door and whip Leo's ass like he was her own child. She'd beat down a few bitches in her lifetime, so that was nothing new. Patrice and Monique grew up right next door to each other in the St. Bernard housing projects which was how their kids met each other. Leo and Keller were young kids, so their little childhood crush was cute back in the day. They used to hold hands while walking to school and stay out on the porch talking all night. That was before Leo started hanging with the wrong crowd. He and Keller drifted apart because he couldn't seem to stay out of trouble. It wasn't until they got older that they reconnected and got into a serious relationship. Keller had gone to school and was doing well for herself by then. Unfortunately the same couldn't be said for Leo. He was still the same person that he was when they were younger. Nothing had changed, but his age. He still sold drugs and hung with the same bums that he ran with when they lived in the projects. Patrice was tired of bailing him out of jail, so she let him go his own way. She had three other kids that she had to worry about.

"Baby, I'm sorry. Just open the door so we can talk," Leo pleaded. He'd changed up his attitude just that fast, but Keller was used to that.

"Why? So you can hit me again?" Keller screamed.

"Don't fall for that bullshit girl. I guess he'll be saying that you can hit him back next," Patrice said knowing her son all too well.

"I apologize for that, but I was upset. If it'll make you feel better you can hit me back," Leo said making his mother's prediction come true.

"I knew it!" Patrice yelled triumphantly. Leo was definitely his father's child.

"Is Leandra there?" Keller asked referring to Leo's sister.

"No, I'm here alone. Call Monique and let her come over there and beat his ass," Patrice yawned into the receiver.

"Okay Pat. I know you're tired, so I'll talk to you later," Keller said before they disconnected.

She heard what her mother-in-law had said, but there was no way in hell that she was calling her mother. Monique was a petite woman with a pretty face, but she was a force to be reckoned with. Growing up with mostly brothers had her tough as iron. She was as feminine as they came until it was time to fight. The beast came out of her quickly, especially behind her only two daughters or only grandchild. If she thought that Leo had laid a finger on one of her babies she would be at their door with her gun out in minutes. Keller and her sister Kia grew up without a father, but that didn't mean a thing. Monique had their backs and her brothers had hers.

"Man, open the fucking door!" Leo boomed letting his abusive side resurface.

"You better get your bipolar ass away from this door. I'm about to call Mo and tell her to come and get me," Keller said referring to her mother by her nickname.

"That's how you gon' do me Keller. Why you gotta call Mo? We can work this shit out on our own. Why you gotta try to get me killed?" He asked sounding hurt.

He hated when Keller threatened to call her mama or her sister's boyfriend on him. He wasn't a scary nigga, but some battles just weren't worth fighting. He'd seen Mo go toe to toe with grown men and walk away without a scratch. She was so tiny and quiet that most people often underestimated her. She didn't go looking for trouble, but she handled it when it came to her. He would definitely be pushing up daisies if she found out that he'd hit her daughter.

"We don't have nothing to work out. I'm done for good this time," Keller said trying to convince herself as well as him.

"So you don't love me no more Keller?" Leo asked pitifully.

"You damn sure don't love me. If you did you wouldn't keep putting your hands on me. You better leave before Mo gets here. I just sent her a text to pick me up," Keller lied.

"I love you baby. Call me when you get to Mo's house so we can talk," Leo begged right before he grabbed his keys and left. He was sure that Keller had never told her mother about their fights before because Mo had never confronted him. He still didn't want to take that chance so he left just in case she made good on one of her threats. As soon as Keller heard the front door close, she dialed her sister Kia's number. She hated to call so late and wake her niece up, but she needed a ride and she hated cabs. She only prayed that her sister's boyfriend Jaden wasn't home.

Chapter 2

"Ahh," Kia moaned softly as Jaden's tongue slipped in and out of her wetness with ease. He had both of her legs planted on his shoulders as he used his mouth as a weapon. The constant ringing of her phone threatened to kill her vibe, but she tried her best to tune it out.

"Come get up here," Jaden said when he finally came up for air and laid down on his back. Kia wasted no time following his command. She was exhausted from the vicious tongue lashing that he put on her, but she had to handle her business.

"Shit," Jaden hissed as soon as Kia slid down his erect pole. His eyes lowered to slits right before they rolled up and behind his head. He slapped Kia on her ass and she already knew the routine. Whenever she was on top, Jaden expected her to do all the work while he laid back and enjoyed the ride. After planting her feet firmly on the mattress, Kia bounced up and down just like she knew he liked her to. As good as Jaden felt, the ringing of her phone was ruining the mood.

"Jaden wait, I need to answer the phone. Something might be wrong," Kia announced.

"Answer it then," Jaden replied huskily, never opening his eyes.

"Okay," Kia replied as she tried to get off of him.

"I didn't tell you to stop," Jaden said pulling her back down.

"Well how am I gonna answer the phone?" Kia asked.

He finally popped his eyes open and stood to his feet. He never once broke their connection as he walked her over to the dresser and grabbed her phone, handing it to her.

"Now finish handling your business," Jaden demanded as he laid back down in the bed with her still on top.

"You want me to answer the phone and ride you at the same time?" Kia asked just to be clear.

"Multitask," Jaden said as he slapped her ass again to encourage her to keep moving.

Kia laughed, but that was out of the question. She would never be able to concentrate on whoever was on the phone because Jaden had her full attention at the moment. Besides, they both made too much noise for her to do that. She just hoped that Jaden didn't want to do his normal three hours or more sex session so that she could get back with whoever kept calling her. Deciding to speed things up, Kia quickened her pace and had Jaden tapping out a few minutes later. He was high and tipsy, so he turned over and was snoring lightly in no time at all. Kia got up from the bed and took a quick shower. Afterwards, she grabbed a warm soapy towel and proceeded to wipe Jaden off.

"Thanks baby," Jaden mumbled before he drifted off once again. When she cleaned up her mess, Kia checked on her daughter before checking the missed calls on her phone. She panicked a little when she saw that her sister Keller had called more than ten times. She wasted no time calling her back all the while praying that everything was alright.

"What took you so long to answer?" Keller snapped when she answered the phone.

"Bitch it's after one in the morning. People are usually sleeping at this hour," Kia replied with just as much attitude.

"I'm sorry sis, but I really need you right now," Keller said.

"What's wrong?" Kia asked as she sat up at her kitchen table.

Keller was older than Kia by eleven months, but she always acted as her sister's protector. Their father was killed in a drug deal gone wrong when Mo was pregnant with Kia, so it was always the three of them looking out for each other. Mo had brothers who acted as father figures, but they weren't good influences. They were involved in the dope game, but not as heavily as they were when they were younger. Mo's two sisters didn't come around too often, so she was closer with her brothers.

"Me and Leo got into it. I need to get away from his ass for a few days," Keller said interrupting her sister's thoughts.

"Did he hit you?" Kia questioned. When Keller paused she already knew the answer.

"No," she lied effortlessly.

"Stop lying Keller. You're protecting his ass now?" Kia yelled.

"No, he didn't hit me. We just argued and he left," she continued to lie.

"Yeah right. If that was the case you wouldn't be trying to leave home."

"Can you come get me or not?" Keller asked her sister.

"No, Jaden will go crazy if I leave out of here this late. I know you don't want to, but you'll have to call a cab or call Mo," Kia answered.

"You know damn well I'm not calling Mo and I hate catching cabs. It's not like I live that far from you. Can't you sneak out and get me? You'll be back before he even misses you."

"Seriously Keller? You've know Jaden just as long as I have. Do you really think that's possible?" Kia questioned.

Keller didn't answer because she knew how Jaden was. He never put his hands on Kia, but he came up with crazy and unique ways to express his anger. He and Kia had been off and on since she was younger. He and Kia broke up every other month, but they always found their way right back to each other. Jaden was Kia's first everything which was how she got pregnant at sixteen and became a teenaged mother at seventeen. Their daughter Jaylynn was ten years old and she made sure that her father didn't stay away for too long. Kia and Jaylynn were his hearts and everybody knew it, no matter how many times they broke up. Thanks to him, Keller was able to get a job doing what she loved and was certified to do. Jaden was a barber at his brother Bryce's shop and he talked his brother into hiring her. Keller was the only nail tech there and Bryce loved the new business that she generated. After a few months, he knocked down a wall and gave Keller her own little area. It was then that she decided to start doing make-up in the shop as well. Thanks to some of Jaden's family members, the shop stayed jumping with lots of entertainment.

"Let me call a cab, but you better stay on the phone with me until I pull up," Keller demanded.

She hated cabs ever since a girl that she went to beauty school with was raped and killed by a cab driver a few years ago. Keller had just seen her get into the cab right after class and that was the last time anybody saw her alive. Her body was found in a field not too far from her house the following morning. The cab driver was caught a few weeks later trying to go back to Mexico.

Keller had been leery of cabs and cab drivers ever since that dreadful day.

"Okay, I will," Kia promised her.

She waited on the line until her sister called the cab. Kia laughed when her sister sent her a picture of the cab with its license plate visible. Keller asked the driver a million questions from the time he picked her up until they were pulling up in front of Kia's house. Kia opened the door and helped her sister with her bags. She could see that Keller had been crying, but that wasn't all that she saw.

"Why'd you lie to me?" Kia asked once she and her sister were in her spare bedroom.

"I didn't lie to you about anything," Keller swore.

"You told me that Leo didn't hit you."

"He didn't," Keller yelled in aggravation.

"Then why is your lip busted? That lipstick ain't as good as you think it is," Kia observed.

Keller turned her head and avoided making eye contact with her sister. Kia already didn't like Leo and she didn't want to give her any more reasons than she already had. Kia knew that she and Leo had fought in the past, but Keller had her believing that it hadn't happened again.

"I'm good Kia," Keller replied.

"Now I know why you didn't wanna call Mo. I need to call and tell her how Leo has been putting his hands on you," Kia threatened even though she would never do it.

"Why would you do that? You don't see me calling Mo telling her all of you and Jaden's business."

"Jaden doesn't put his hands on me either."

"Yeah, but he's a cheater. Call and tell Mo about that girl that's been stalking you because of your man," Keller snapped angrily.

During one of Kia and Jaden's break-ups, he hooked up with a certified nut case named Tori. The girl claimed to be pregnant by him at one time before she supposedly miscarried. Keller didn't know what Jaden had done to Tori, but she was a lunatic. She showed up at the shop just about every other week and she even followed Kia from work a few times. Jaden choked her crazy ass up so many times, but nothing seemed to keep her away. He even paid his cousin and some of her friends to jump her, but Tori still didn't get the point. Keller assumed it was because he was still messing with her, but he swore to Kia that he wasn't.

"Bitch don't even try to come for me. I'm not saying that Jaden is perfect. He does his dirt, but most of the time we're not even together when he messes with other females. Not only does Leo cheat on you, but he beats your ass while he's doing it," Kia yelled shaking her sister from her daydream.

She regretted the words as soon as they left her mouth, but it was too late to take them back. Keller was always trying to throw shade at her when she didn't have any room to talk. She hated arguing with her sister, but she needed to let her know a few things.

"Thanks for letting me crash in your spare bedroom. I'll ask Tessa to pick me up later and stay with her for a while," Keller said referring to her friend.

"You don't have to leave Keller. We have differences all the time, but you always have a place to stay as long as I have a house. I'm sorry about what I said," Kia apologized.

"Me too," Keller smiled. She hated arguing with her sister, but they couldn't stay mad with each other for long. She had lots of friends, but none of them could compare to Kia. Her friend Tessa came close, but there was no one else like her sister. After telling her sister the entire truth about what happened, Keller took a hot shower and crashed a few minutes later. Leo was still blowing her phone up, but she had no words for him. At least she didn't for now.

Chapter 3

"You know you're welcomed to stay here as long as you want to if you ever get tired of being at Kia's," Tessa said as she and Keller ate the pizza that she'd just ordered.

"Thanks girl, but I'll probably be going back home soon. Leo is about to lose his damn mind. I've been gone for almost a week," Keller answered through a mouth full of food.

"I wish you would stay gone for good. Leo is cool, but his temper is too bad. He goes off the deep end for nothing at all," Tessa said.

"Don't start Tessa. I hear enough of that from my sister. I'm not saying that Leo is right, but no relationship is perfect. I've put my hands on him more times than I can count, so we're both at fault," Keller said making Tessa shake her head.

She and Keller had met each other over five years ago, but they lost contact with each other after just a short while. Tessa had gone to school out of town and she and Keller kind of drifted apart. Once she got her degree in Business Administration, she moved back home to New Orleans to work at her family's construction business. She thought about Keller a lot, but she didn't know how to get in touch with her. Her number wasn't the same and she didn't know much about her family at the time. About three months after she'd been back home, Tessa had a date with a man that she'd been interested in for a while. She was horrified when she got stood up by her hair stylist and she didn't know what to do. She started to cancel the date until she saw a billboard on the bridge advertising hair, nails and makeup at a salon called So-Xclusive. When she saw that walk-ins were welcomed, she decided to take a chance and see if she could be seen. She was shocked, but pleasantly surprised when she found out that Keller was the nail tech and make-up artist. Not to mention her hair came out better than her stylist ever did it. Keller did a wonderful job on her nails and make-up as well. She made another appointment with the hair stylist, Co-Co, and she'd been going to him every week since then. Co-Co was hilarious so Tessa usually ended up spending the entire day there when she did go.

"As long as you're okay, that's all that matters to me," Tessa finally spoke up right as her nieces came strolling in.

"We're done eating auntie," her oldest niece Tia said.

"Okay boo, throw y'all plates away and go watch TV," Tessa instructed.

"What time is our daddy picking us up?" Her other niece Talia asked.

"He should be here in a little while," Tessa answered.

"Tessa's older brother, Tigga had three daughters, but she was only watching two of them. Actually, their mother was supposed to be watching them, but she dropped them off to Tessa when it was time for her to go to work.

"Where's the baby girl?" Keller asked referring to her two year old niece Amari.

"She's with her nanny. Tigga gon' be pissed when he find that out," Tessa replied.

"Why? He don't like her to go by her nanny?" Keller questioned.

"It's not that. He just feels like her nanny builds bridges between Amari and the other two girls. He don't like nobody doing for one without doing for the others."

"I don't blame him. They're kids, they don't understand stuff like that."

"And she's such a sickly little thing. She has asthma and epilepsy. She hasn't had a seizure in a while, but she don't need to be sleeping by everybody's house like that. Not to mention how dirty she be looking when she comes back home," Tessa said.

"That's a damn shame. Where is their mama?" Keller asked.

"That nasty bitch is probably at a club or with her trifling friends. My mama had them overnight and she never came to pick them up. She knew that my mama had to work today and she's not even answering her phone," Tessa fussed.

"She's pretty, but she don't really look like your brother's type. That nigga looks like Boris Kodjoe with a tight fade," Keller said making Tessa laugh. Tessa was on the thick side, but she was cute and had her own little style. Her short hair complimented her round baby face and caramel skin tone. Keller always joked and called her a plus sized Kerry Washington because of her full, pouty lips.

"My brother is handsome, but he got caught up with a hood rat. Her looks is all that she got going for her because she's ghetto as hell. Bitch probably turkey basted my nieces right into her womb," Tessa replied making Keller fall over with laughter.

"Bitch you stupid," Keller sang.

"I'm serious. I wish you would have met him first. That bitch Anaya ain't right."

"Baby if I wasn't with Leo, I would give her a run for her money," Keller swore.

"How about we hook Anaya up with Leo and you and Tigger can get together," Tessa suggested. Keller laugher her off, but she was serious.

"Don't tempt me with his fine ass. I'll leave Leo in my dust," Keller replied.

Tessa was always telling her that her brother asked about her, but they were both in a relationship. It didn't make sense to try to pursue something with him knowing that it wouldn't or couldn't go anywhere.

"She know what she's doing though. Tigga is big on family and she's using my nieces to keep him around. Our daddy abandoned us and he doesn't want to do that to his girls. Thank God for our mama and grandparents," Tessa replied.

"Your daddy is crazy. He came from money, but would rather live on the streets.

"That's what drugs will do to you," Tessa shrugged.

Tessa's father, Terrell was an only child and she and her brother were his only two kids. Tessa's grandfather, who she and her brother called Bo, was the founder and owner of Coleman Construction where her father worked from the time he was old enough to get a job. They started out with one construction site and expanded to eight over the years. It was always known that Terrell would be the one who ran the family business when his father retired, but things didn't turn out the way they planned it. Terrell and their mother Christy were married and lived a good life with their kids until he started to become abusive. Everything that Christy did resulted in a beating until she'd finally had enough. Tigga and Tessa were too young for her to have them in the violent environment that Terrell had created. After being beaten almost daily for months, Christy packed up her kids and moved in with her in-laws. They were pissed at the man that Terrell had become, but they wanted Christy and their grandkids to be comfortable and safe. Terrell continued to work at his father's business for a few months after he and Christy separated, but his family started noticing some changes in him. Some days he wouldn't show up for work and nobody would hear from him for hours. Then his father started to notice that checks were being written to Terrell from the company's account that he didn't authorize. When Bo confronted his son, he became defensive and stormed off of the job. After a few weeks of being away, Terrell came back to work like it was nothing. It just so happened that the day he returned was the day that the job was taking mandatory drug tests. Usually he didn't have to do it, but his father demanded he take one that time. It broke his family's heart when his drug test came back positive. At the time, Bo didn't know what kind of drugs his son indulged in. After a few months of ups and downs, he soon found out that crack had become his son's drug of choice. Apparently some woman that he cheated on Christy with had introduced him to it. They started out smoking it in their cigarettes, but the glass pipe replaced that soon after. That explained his abusive behavior and his lack of commitment to the company that he helped to build. Bo and his wife tried everything to help their only child. They spent thousands on rehab, but it was all done in vain. Terrell's addiction only got worse and it seemed like there was no coming back from that. He went months without seeing his wife and kids until Christy finally gave up and divorced him. Bo helped her get a house and she got a job working nights as a dispatcher for the police department to take care of her kids. Bo offered her financial assistance, but Christy preferred her independence. Being a single mother was hard, but with the help of her now ex-in-laws she was able to survive. Terrell being addicted to drugs affected them all in some way, but none more than Tigga. He was only eight years old at the time and he looked up to his father. He went from seeing him every day to not seeing him at all. Terrell would make promises to him, but he never fulfilled them. Tigga used to sit at the window for hours waiting for a visit that would never come. After a while, he stopped caring about Terrell and gravitated more towards his grandfather. Bo knew that his son was a lost cause, so he started grooming his only grandson to run the business. As soon as Tigga made twenty-one, Bo handed the multi-million dollar company over to him and he'd been running it ever since. He was now twenty-nine years old and making more money than men twice his age. Half of the staff had to be replaced because they gave Tigga hell in the beginning. Most of the men had been working for the company longer than he had been born. They had trouble taking orders from someone who could have been their child. Tigga had his work cut out for him, but he handled business like the boss that he was. After getting order in his company, business had been better than ever. He gave Tessa a job working in the office and paid her a nice salary to do it. Tessa was only twenty-five years old, but she was doing pretty well for herself too.

"Did he ever buy a house yet?" Keller asked pulling Tessa away from her thoughts of the past.

"Hell no! My mama said she dares him to buy a house with Anaya's trifling ass," Tessa replied.

"But why? It don't seem like he's going anywhere. You said yourself that he's staying around for his daughters."

"He is for now, but I can tell that he's getting tired of her. Her only job is to take care of their kids and she can't even do that right. She's always dropping them off to somebody so she can run the streets with her friends. She gon' lose a good man behind them hoes that she hang with," Tessa concluded.

"I swear I don't understand this relationship shit sometimes. Leo got a damn good woman in me, but the ghetto birds in the clubs seems to be what he's attracted to. Tigga seems like a dream come true, but Anaya would rather hang with her friends than keep her man happy. That's just crazy," Keller said shaking her head.

"I'm telling you Keller, you and my brother would make the perfect couple," Tessa said once again.

Keller only smiled, but she didn't reply. She would be lying if she said that Tessa's brother wasn't the full package, but watching was all that she could do. They were both in relationships, so getting together was out of the question. Leo wasn't what she would have considered a prize, but she still loved him anyway.

"Speaking of your new man. This is him calling me now," Tessa teased her.

"Let me start straightening up so you don't have this to do when I leave," Keller offered as she left Tessa to talk in peace.

She grabbed the pizza boxes and paper plates and put them all away. It was late and almost time for her to go home. Tessa was going to bring her, but she didn't know which home she wanted to go to. She was missing Leo like crazy, but she didn't want to hear Kia's mouth if she went back home. Then again, she was grown and didn't have to answer to anyone. Suddenly the decision became easier. She was going home to her man no matter how Kia felt about it.

Chapter 4

"I'm on my way. I need to stop at the store right quick. You need something?" Tigga asked his sister over the phone.

"No I'm good. I gave the girls a bath and fed them, so they can go straight to bed," Tessa replied.

"Good looking out lil sis. I appreciate you," Tigga said before they disconnected.

He tried calling Anaya for the third time, but his call went unanswered yet again. That was the bullshit that had him not wanting to be with her anymore. Anaya was cool in the beginning, but she got way too comfortable after the babies came. Tigga knew that he made his mistake when he confided in her about his commitment to keeping his family together. He refused to turn his back on his girls like his father did to him and his sister. If that meant staying with their mother even when he didn't want to, he would just have to deal. Anaya was the type of chick who would use her kids as leverage if she couldn't have her way. He saw that for himself when they broke up once before. He didn't see his girls for over a month until they got back together. His mother tried to get him to take it to court, but he didn't want to bring his kids through all of that. Being the perfect father meant everything to him since he didn't get to experience that for himself. He wanted his girls to be proud of him and he worked hard to make that happen. Still, something had to give because he couldn't take being with Anaya much longer.

"Let me hold something Tigga," a man said as soon as he got out of his truck and walked up to the front door of the corner store.

"You'll never buy no drugs with my hard earned money," Tigga replied as he bypassed him and walked inside.

Being that he grew up in the area, he knew mostly all of the men who hung around there. That's why he wasn't surprised when the man got up from the crate that he was sitting on and followed him inside.

"I'm not trying to buy no dope. I'm hungry, I want a hot sausage sandwich," he replied to Tigga's back.

"Order it and I'll pay for it. You know I'm not putting no money in your hands," Tigga said as he continued to look around for some snacks for his girls.

"Alright, thanks Tigga," he said as he rushed off to go order his meal for the day.

"Order me one too Joe, he got it," Tigga heard an all too familiar voice reply from the back of the store.

Joe turned around and looked at Tigga before he made the wrong move. He didn't want to jeopardize his free meal by ordering more than he was told to.

"Order your shit and that's all. Fuck what anybody else is saying," Tigga snapped as he continued to move about in the store.

Joe hurried to the counter and placed his order before Tigga went off and changed his mind. He knew how his attitude could go from calm to crazy in a matter of seconds.

"It's like that son?" Terrell walked over to Tigga and asked.

"Don't call me no fucking son. Call me Tigga just like the rest of these niggas out here. You ain't no different than nobody else," Tigga snapped.

"I'm your daddy so that makes me different from the rest," Terrell yelled angrily.

"Man Rell, you better get the fuck on with that bullshit," Tigga said as he walked to the counter.

"Chill out Terrell," Joe said trying to keep a situation from occurring.

"Nah, fuck that! This nigga let that lil money go to his head and now he feels like he can disrespect me," Terrell said angrily.

"Get your facts straight nigga. I got a lot of money and I'm the same person today that I've been from day one. I just don't fuck with you," Tigga laughed as he pulled a huge knot of money from his pocket just to prove his point.

Terrell eyed the money nervously like he wanted to snatch it and run, but he knew better. His son was tall and muscular just like he was back in the day. Tigga was handsome and held most of the features that he had before the drugs took his looks away from him. His daughter Tessa was a beautiful caramel colored replica of his ex-wife, but his son was all him. Terrell knew that nigga hated him, but he still didn't like the way he treated him. He might have deserved it, but it was embarrassing how his son disregarded him in front of other people.

"You talking like I don't know how it feels to be paid. Nigga you know when I had my shit together nobody couldn't touch me even if they wanted to," Terrell said after a few minutes of silence.

"This nigga is crazy," Tigga chuckled ignoring his father. "Get your stuff so I can pay for it Joe. I need to go get my kids and go home."

Joe grabbed his sandwich and something to drink and met Tigga at the cash register. Terrell was still mumbling some bullshit under his breath, but his son just ignored him. Terrell couldn't help but to feel like his son was living the life that was intended for him had it not been for the drugs. He knew that he'd hurt his wife and kids when he abandoned them for months at a time, but the drugs had a strong hold on him. Tigga used to be his shadow at one point. He couldn't go anywhere without his son begging to follow. Now it was as if he never existed in his life at all. Terrell had seen his granddaughters in passing, but he was never formally introduced to any of them. Terrell hung out in their old hood and Tigga still had friends in the area. He would often stop by places that his father hung out at, but most of the time he acted like he didn't even know him. That was hurtful, but his son didn't seem to care.

"Good looking Tigga. I owe you a car wash when you come back through," Joe promised as he walked out with his food.

"I want that too nigga. Don't play dumb when I roll up on your ass either," Tigga said while getting into his car.

"I got you," Joe said right before Tigga pulled off. When his phone started ringing, he frowned at the screen as if the caller could see him.

"Why the fuck you didn't answer your phone when I kept calling?" Tigga snapped when he answered the phone for Anaya.

"I'm sorry baby, but I left it on the charger at my mama's house. I went to bring her to run some errands and I forgot to get it," Anaya said.

"You full of shit Anaya. You out there running the streets knowing that my mama had to work today. She had to drop the kids off by Tessa because you didn't answer the phone."

"I didn't know that she had to work today. Tell Tessa that I'll be there to get them in a few minutes," she replied.

"Don't even worry about it. I'm on my way over there already," Tigga said angrily.

"Okay, I'll see y'all at home in a little while," Anaya replied.

Tigga hung up the phone in her face without bothering to reply. Anya wasn't even worth an argument, so he didn't bother giving her one. He turned his music up and listened to Young Jeezy spit some fire lyrics as he headed to his sister's house. A little over ten minutes later, Tigga was pulling up to Tessa's house. He rang the doorbell and smiled when he heard his daughter's getting excited about his arrival. As soon as the door was opened, they ran up to him and jumped into his arms.

"Y'all missed me?" Tigga asked his girls as she carried them back inside.

"Yeah, we missed you. Did you bring us something?" His oldest daughter asked.

"You already know I did," he answered as he put them down on the floor.

That was a daily routine for them that they looked forward to. No matter where he went, he made sure to pick something up for his girls, even if it was just a snack from the corner store. It was the little things that made kids happy. He just wished his father had thought like that when he and Tessa were younger.

"Y'all go put your shoes on and get your bags," Tessa ordered her nieces.

"Amari must be sleep," Tigga assumed.

"Nope, she was never here. Anaya didn't tell you? She's with her nanny," Tessa revealed.

"Her stupid ass didn't tell me nothing. She was by mama's house yesterday. When did she go over there?"

"I don't even know," Tessa answered.

Tigga was about to reply until something else caught his attention. His voice got caught in his throat when he saw Keller's sexy ass come into view.

"Hey Tyler," Keller said calling him by his real name.

"What's up?" Tigga said while looking her curvaceous body over and licking his lips. Keller was built like a coke bottle and he wouldn't mind taking a sip. He knew that she had a nigga, but that didn't mean a damn thing to him. He was always asking his sister about her, but he was ready to make a move on his own. If her body wasn't enough to have him drooling at the mouth, her face completed the package. Keller reminded him of Jada Pinkett in her younger days, but her hair wasn't as short.

"It sounds so weird hearing somebody call him by his real name," Tessa chuckled interrupting his stare down of her friend.

"I think Tyler is a cute name. Besides, I know your mama didn't name him after a Winnie the Pooh character," Keller laughed.

"That's where she got it from, but he just spells it different. He hates his real name though," Tessa replied like her brother wasn't standing right there.

"I'm sorry, I didn't know that," Keller apologized while looking over at him.

"Nah ma, it's cool. I like the way it sounds when you say it," Tigga winked making her blush.

Tessa just stood back and watched how her best friend and brother stared each other down like she wasn't even standing there. She knew that the attraction was there, but they had to get rid of their significant others before they could do anything about it.

"We're ready to go daddy," Tia announced when she walked into the room.

"Alright," Tigga replied as he pulled his gaze away from Keller and grabbed their bags.

"Bye," his daughters said as they gave their auntie and Keller a hug.

"Bye pretty girls," Keller said as she hugged them back.

"Wait Tigga, let me grab my purse so I can walk out with you. I have to bring Keller home," Tessa said as she attempted to walk away.

"I can bring her home. Where you live at?" Tigga asked while turning to Keller.

"In Gretna," she replied giving him the address to where she and Leo lived.

They were getting into his silver Hummer and pulling off soon after. Keller was a little nervous at first, but Tigga made her feel very comfortable. He was easy to talk to and their conversation flowed effortlessly. They talked about their jobs amongst other things before he pulled up to her apartment complex.

"Thanks for the ride Tyler, I mean Tigga," Keller said when she opened the car door to get out.

"Nah, don't change up on me. You can call me Tyler," he replied with a sexy smile that caused a flood between her legs.

"Okay, thanks again," Keller smiled back.

"Wait," Tigga yelled before she closed the door and walked away.

"What's up?" Keller asked.

"Here," he said handing her his phone. "Put your number in here. I already know you got a man and you know what's up with me, so there's no need to state the obvious."

"You're not shy are you?" Keller smirked as she put her name and number in his phone.

"We're grown. There's no need for all that," Tigga replied.

"Good night," Keller said as she closed the door and walked to her building.

Tigga watched her until she was safely inside before he pulled off. Keller was happy that Leo wasn't home because she was smiling from ear to ear when she walked through the door. She couldn't believe that Tigga had asked for her number, but she didn't hesitate to give it to him. She didn't give a damn about Leo or Anaya. When he called, she was going to make it her business to answer him.

Chapter 5

"That nigga be straight handling your ass. But you be quick to curse me out if I say the wrong thing," Rich said while looking at Anaya in disgust.

Tigga had just called and went off on her about something, but he couldn't make out what was being said. And just like always, he hung up the phone in her face once he said what he had to say. He had already called a few minutes ago and went off on her for not picking the kids up from his mama's house.

"Mind your fucking business nigga. Get up and put your clothes on so I can drop you off home," Anaya snapped in aggravation.

"See what I'm saying? That nigga talk crazy to you, but you don't tell him shit. I guess he can do that since he got a lil change, huh?" Rich said as he grabbed his clothes from the floor and headed to the bathroom.

"Stupid ass," Anaya mumbled as soon as he slammed the bathroom door.

Messing around with his dumb ass was the reason that she was late picking her girls up from Christy's house in the first place. Tigga was already mad that she didn't pick the girls up, now he was pissed because she let Amari spend the night at her nanny's house. She and Rich usually hooked up at one of his sisters or cousins houses, but he'd finally managed to hustle up enough money to pay for them a room this time. Anaya didn't mean to stay gone so long, but it was nice to be with her boo without worrying about somebody walking in on them. She hated that Rich had heard Tigga going off because that was another thing that he had to throw in her face. He'd been on her back a lot lately about the two of them being together, but she just couldn't do it. Anaya and Rich had grown up together in a trailer park community, but thanks to Tigga she was fortunate enough to get out. Her mother and sisters still lived in the run down area and so did most of Rich's family. She couldn't deny that she was indeed in love with him, but he couldn't provide the life for her that she had become accustomed to living. Leaving him alone wasn't as easy as it should have been because of her feelings for him. She loved Tigga too, but she had history with Rich. He was her first love, but he just wasn't a go getter. He was in jail more than he was free and she just couldn't depend on him to support her and her girls. That's one reason why she was happy that Tigga was the man who she'd started a family with. Without a doubt, she knew that they would always have a roof over their heads and all of their needs would be met. Tigga had his heart set on being a good father, especially since he didn't have one of his own. He was determined to be the opposite of what his father had been to him and Tessa and he had succeeded. Anaya knew that her girls were the only reason why they were still together and she was grateful for that. Tigga would rather put up with being in a relationship with her than to not see his daughters. Anaya had love for both men, but she knew the time would come where she would have to choose. Rich was getting fed up, so it was only a matter of time. If only she could take parts of both men to create the perfect man, all of her troubles would be over. With Tigga's looks and finances combined with the love and history that she had for Rich, she wouldn't have any complaints.

"You ready?" Rich asked interrupting Anaya's thoughts.

"Yeah," she said as she grabbed her purse and stood to her feet.

She was happy that she'd already taken a shower and was dressed by the time she called Tigga back. She was already late enough as it was.

"Here, I'll try to have more for you next week," Rich said as he handed Anaya some money. He frowned when she thumbed through the money to see how much it was.

"Thanks," Anaya said when she counted the eighty dollars that he'd just placed in the palm of her hand.

"You don't appreciate shit! I said I'll have more for you next week," Rich snapped once he saw the look on her face.

"I said thanks. What the fuck do you want me to say?" Anaya snapped.

"It's not what you said, it's the look on your face. I might not be able to give you as much as that other nigga, but my time is coming. As soon as I get my shit straight I'm coming for you and you better be ready," Rich said reciting the same line that he recited whenever they were together.

"I know you're trying baby and I appreciate that," Anaya said with a forced smile.

He didn't know it, but he was helping to prove the point that she was trying to make. She didn't know what the hell he expected her to do with eighty dollars. A trip to Chuck E. Cheese's with her daughters caused twice that much. The only thing rich about him was the nickname that he'd adopted when they were younger. Aside from some bomb ass sex, he couldn't do a damn thing for her. Tigga was bigger and better in the bedroom, but they barely had sex anymore. Once a month was a lot and it was usually over before she really got started. Sex with Tigga wasn't for her pleasure anymore. He basically pounded into her like a crazy person until he came. There was no foreplay or intimacy, just straight fucking to get a nut. His nut because she was never able to get hers. Rich, on the other hand, treated her like fine China. He made her remember why she fell in love with him and why she still was.

"Friday night right?" Rich said referring to the next time they would be seeing each other.

"Yes," Anaya agreed as they walked out of the motel room hand in hand. She got into her truck and started it up while Rich went to turn in the room key. She needed to call her mother, Donna, to put her up on the story that she'd told Tigga just in case he asked her.

"Drop me off at my mama's house baby. I need to go talk to my brother about a few things," Rich said when he got into the car.

"Yeah okay, you can let your brother have your ass back in jail if you want to. I told you that I'm done visiting and sending money to the jail house," Anaya swore.

Just like Rich, his brother Anthony didn't have a hustling bone in his body. They both tried and failed at selling dope, so robbery became their thing. They were even too dumb to do that right because they never went after anybody with real money. They went after the low budget corner hustlers and barely walked away with enough money to pay a bill.

"It's not even like baby. Besides, it's not like it was your money that you were sending me anyway," he looked at her and laughed.

"That's not funny Rich. You go back to jail again and I'm done with you," Anaya promised.

"Girl you ain't going nowhere. You always say that just to scare a nigga. You might sleep next to that nigga every night, but I know who your heart belongs to," Rich said right as they pulled up to the trailer park.

Anaya didn't reply because she knew that he was right. If he hadn't gone to jail for two years once before, she probably would have never even started messing with Tigga. By the time Rich came back home to rekindle what they once had, she was already six months into her pregnancy with her oldest daughter. He was hurt, but that still didn't stop him from wanting to be with her. Even after she had her other daughters he wanted her just the same. He couldn't provide for them like Tigga could, but Rich was willing to do whatever he had to do to try.

"I'll call you later boo. I love you," Anaya said while looking over at Rich.

"I love you too baby. I'll talk to you later," Rich replied right before he kissed her and got out of the car.

Anaya was barely out of the parking lot before her phone started ringing. She didn't even have to look at the screen to know who the caller was.

"Hey ma," Anaya said when she answered the phone.

"Don't hey ma me. Your stupid ass is still messing with that loser, huh?" Donna yelled into the phone.

"Excuse me, but I'm grown just in case you forgot," Anaya snapped angrily.

It was no secret to Rich or anybody else about how Donna felt about the two of them being together. She didn't have anything against Rich, but she knew that her daughter could do better. With skin the color of smooth dark chocolate, Anaya could pass for a model with her slender build and exotic features. Donna often referred to her daughter as a dark skinned Zoe Saldana, but Anaya's attitude wouldn't get her too far in life. She had a good man at home, but she would rather throw it all away behind a bum just because she had a little history with him. Rich and his entire family disgusted her, but her daughter seemed to love everything about them. Although they lived in the same trailer park, Donna made sure to stay her distance. She wanted whatever her daughter and Rich had to be over, but she knew that it probably never would be. Anaya was a twenty-seven year old fool in love.

"I know you're grown, but I also know that you're stupid too. You're riding his broke ass around in a sixty thousand dollar truck that your man paid for and he couldn't even fill the gas tank up if you needed him too," Donna fussed.

"It's nobody's business, but he just gave me some money for your information," Anaya said taking his side.

"Yeah right. I bet it wasn't over one hundred dollars if he did," her mother replied making her feel stupid.

"Is that why you called me or did you need something else?" Anaya asked her.

"I saw you drop that scrub off and that's why I called. And did you know that your daughter was back here?" Donna asked.

"Amari is with her nanny," she snapped in aggravation.

"Her nanny, huh? Well her nanny keeps her dirty just like she does with the rest of them kids over there. I got a good mind to go over there and give her a bath. And I thought Tigga said he didn't want her over there no more anyway."

"Tigga ain't the only one who can make decisions for Amari. You know that me and Erica have been friends for years. I know that she's gonna take good care of my baby. She always does," Anaya said.

"You're only saying that because she's Rich's cousin. That bitch ain't taking care of your damn baby. Got her walking around here looking like a garbage pail kid," Donna argued.

"Alright ma, I just got home so I'll talk to you later," Anaya said as she whipped her Cayenne Porsche into her assigned parking spot.

"Don't expect me to keep lying for you Anaya. You better stop trying to cheat on your future for your past. That shit is gonna blow up in your face. Rich can't give you nothing but a stiff dick and a bunch of broken promises. You should have had enough of that when y'all were together."

"Bye mama," Anaya said as she wiped the tears before they fell from her eyes.

She didn't expect her mother to understand how she felt. Donna wanted her to have a good life and she felt that Tigga was the one who could provide it for her. Donna didn't even like Tigga like that, but she loved his money. Anaya just hated feeling like she was a burden on the man who was supposed to love her. It would have been easier if she had her own money, but she was assed out if it wasn't for Tigga. Getting child support wasn't out of the question, but he would probably get full custody before he gave her a dime. Maybe it was cheaper to keep her, which was why he probably hadn't kicked her to the curb yet. His mother and sister hated her, but they tolerated her for the kids sake just like Tigga did.

"Hey," Anaya said when she walked into their condo.

"Hey," Tigga said dryly returning her greeting. He was posted up in the sitting room that had basically become his bedroom since he rarely slept in their bed anymore. He had a day bed in there with a huge TV and mini fridge. Tigga smoked from sun up to sun down so he never let his girls go anywhere near the room. They would probably get high just from walking in there.

"Are the girls sleeping?" Anaya asked trying to make small talk.

"Yeah and you need to make it your business to get Amari back home tomorrow. You already know how I feel about her going over there. She's picking up on too many bad habits."

Tigga wasn't lying about that. Amari was at the age where she repeated everything, especially curse words. She didn't even call them mama and daddy anymore. They were Naya and Tigga because that's what she heard other people say. Her nanny Erica had a foul mouth so there was no secret as to where most of her bad language came from. Erica's kids were bad as hell too, so Amari was really getting an ear full.

"I'll pick her up in the morning," Anaya promised as she turned to walk away. "Are you coming to bed?"

"I'm already in my bed," he replied never taking his eyes off of the TV.

"Wow," Anaya said as she closed the door and went upstairs to their room.

After taking another quick shower, she got into her bed and prepared to sleep alone just like she been doing for the past few months.

Chapter 6

"Bitch what's wrong with you?" Co-Co asked Keller as soon as she walked into the shop. He was finishing up with a sew-in, but the shop was empty other than that. It wasn't even eight in the morning and Mo was her first client of the day. She wasn't due until ten, but Keller had to get her mind right before she saw her mother. Mo could just look at her and Kia and tell when something wasn't right. She just needed to get away from Leo, so the shop was the only place that she thought of. It had been a month since their last episode, but he was acting a fool once again. Keller confronted him about a chick that he was supposedly messing with and he tried to turn everything around on her. Usually she would have left it alone, but the bitch started playing on her phone making things worse. Leo swore that he didn't know who it was, but the girl damn sure knew a lot about him. They argued all night and Keller ended up sleeping on the sofa. She didn't even wait for him to wake up and drop her off at work. She woke up at the crack of dawn and took the car while he was still sleeping. She didn't give a damn if he had something to do or not.

"Long night, and no, I don't wanna talk about it," she said cutting him off before he even asked. She knew that she was about to get cussed out, but she didn't care.

"Baby you need to walk back outside and check that attitude at the door. You bitches kill me coming in here with attitudes because those niggas be making y'all mad at home."

"What does Leo have to do with anything?" Keller asked as she started to set up her work area. She never got offended by anything that Co-Co said because she already knew how he was. He spoke his mind and he'd been like that since the first day they met.

"He obviously has everything to do with it. You was all smiles for the past month when things were going good. You was getting the dick regularly and all was right with the world," Co-Co said making his client giggle.

"Everything is still right with the world. As long as you and Dwight are good is all that matters," Keller smirked knowing that he was going to get hyped.

"Baby trust and believe that me and my man are doing fine. That's y'all love sick hoes coming in here with all these problems. Jaden got this psychotic bitch stalking him and Kia. You got Leo's ugly ass popping you upside your head every time you go inside a minute after eight. Even Brian got women troubles coming through here every other day," he said referring to the other barber who was also Jaden's brother.

"Now you're wrong for that. Don't call my man ugly," Keller replied.

"Bitch I was trying to be nice. Leo looks like somebody built his ass from the ground up in a science lab. But I know for sure that his dick game is on point. The ugly ones always put it down the best. As pretty as you are nobody will ever understand why you're with him, but I get it. That nigga is probably rearranging your organs every time he hit it," Co-Co said as he removed the cape from around his client so that she could leave.

"I hate you," Keller said as she cracked up laughing. She had to admit that Leo wasn't much to look at, but he dressed nice and had confidence that was through the roof.

"You can hate me, but you have to love the truth. I'm telling it like it is."

"What about Kia and Jaden? He's cute and she's sprung off of him too. What's the reason behind that?" Keller inquired.

"Jaden is a rare case. He's handsome and he lays the pipe right. When you get it like that you have to hold on for dear life. They got a few niggas out here like that, but trust me when I say that they're all taken. That's why that crazy bitch Tori is going nutty behind him."

"You got an answer for everything Dr. Phil," Keller laughed.

"Call me what you want, but I keep you bitches lives in order around here. Bryce is gonna fire everybody if he ever finds out what goes on at his shop during the day."

He wasn't lying about that. Bryce and the other tattoo artists worked late nights, so Co-Co ran things during the day. Every week something popped off, but Bryce never got wind of it. Aside from Jaden's crazy stalker, Leo and Keller got into it all the time. Then there were times where the customers had it out and a few fights had to be broken up as a result. Brian had chicks fighting over him all the time and they always came to the shop with their drama. Bryce was laid back and he didn't tolerate foolishness of any kind at his place of business.

"I know," Keller agreed right as a text message came through on her phone.

Her face lit up and a smiled instantly formed on her face when she read the message that Tigga had sent her. Since the night he dropped her off at home they'd been keeping in contact with each other via text messages. He was always sending her good morning or good night messages and she looked forward to them.

"Bitch who got you smiling like that? I know that ain't lil ugly," Co-Co said talking about Leo once again.

"Mind your business," Keller smiled as she typed in her response.

"Every smile got a tear behind it honey. Stop pretending to be happy and make yourself happy for real," Co-Co said as he sat down and waited for his next client to arrive.

"Not this time boo. This smile is genuine," Keller replied right as the door chimed alerting them of a visitor.

She almost pissed in her pants when she saw Leo walk through the door with a frown on his face. She looked out of the window and saw his cousin pulling off letting her know just how he got there.

"Why the fuck you took the car?" Leo yelled as he attempted to walk over to her.

Co-Co was up on his feet in matter of seconds stopping him from going any further.

"Excuse you, but this is a place a business sweetie. It's too early in the morning for the bullshit," Co-Co said putting his hand in Leo's chest to keep him in place.

"Chill out Co-Co. This don't have shit to do with you," Leo barked as he kept his angry glare on Keller.

"It has everything to do with me when you come to my job with it. Now what is it that you want? Maybe I can help you get it."

"Come here Keller," Leo angrily demanded.

Co-Co almost died where he stood when he saw Keller make a move to walk over to him.

"Bitch you better not take another step!" Co-Co yelled making her stop in her tracks.

"Huh?" Keller said looking at him in confusion.

"You're about to walk into a straight up ass whooping. Even Tina had enough sense to run from Ike. What the hell is wrong with you?" Co-Co fussed.

"And you gon' listen to this nigga Keller? Bring your ass here before I come get you," Leo boomed making Keller's heart race with fear.

"And then what?" A female's voice said from the entrance of the shop.

Keller's head snapped around in shock when she heard her mother's voice. Mo's appointment wasn't for another hour, but she came in early to bring her daughter something to eat. She had actually planned to bring it to her house, but she didn't see the car when she drove by there a few minutes ago. Thinking that Keller had an early morning appointment, she decided to go to the shop a little earlier than her appointment time. She was happy that she did when she walked in on Leo screaming at one of her babies.

"Nigga you talking like you're trying to put your hands on my child or something," Mo said as she sat the food down that she had for Keller.

"Nah Mo, you know I wouldn't put my hands on Keller," Leo swore.

"That's not what it sounded like to me. Does he hit you Keller?" She asked while looking at her daughter.

Leo was pleading with his eyes for Keller not to tell her mother the truth. Mo probably wouldn't have done him anything at the moment, but she would have had her brothers handle him if she needed to, and he was sure of that. Co-Co was staring at Keller too, waiting for her to answer Mo's question.

"No, he's never hit me," Keller lied while Leo visibly relaxed.

"This bitch here," Co-Co mumbled while shaking his head.

Keller had covered up so many bruises since she'd been working there, but she always made excuses for why she had them. Everybody knew that Leo was knocking her upside her head, but she refused to keep it real with Mo.

"Okay, so what's the problem? Why was he screaming at you," Mo asked while looking at her daughter and then back at Leo.

"We just had an argument and he came to get the car keys," Keller replied nervously.

She fumbled around in her purse and grabbed the car keys and handed them to Leo.

"Come walk me outside baby," Leo said sounding like a little innocent schoolboy. He'd completely changed his tone since he first walked through the door.

"Boy you deserve an Oscar for that performance," Co-Co said right before he walked to the back of the shop.

"Go ahead and walk him out Keller. I'll be right here waiting on you," Mo said letting Leo know that she wasn't going anywhere.

Leo grabbed Keller's hand and walked her outside to the side parking lot. When they stopped in front of the car, he wrapped his arms around her waist and pulled her close to him.

"You know I love you right?" Leo asked while rubbing her back in a circular motion.

"Yeah," Keller replied as she melted into his embrace.

"I know that I've been acting crazy lately, but I promise you that it won't happen again."

"You always say that Leo. You act right for a few weeks and then you're back to your old ways soon after," Keller replied.

"I know baby, but not this time, I swear," Leo said trying to convince her of his sincerity. He needed to remove any doubts from Keller's mind before she went back into the shop and talked to Mo. He needed her to stay on his team to make sure that she didn't go telling her mother anything that she wasn't supposed to.

"I hear you talking Leo, but I need more than just your broken promises. Your actions speak louder than anything that you could ever say."

"You're right and I'm gonna show you just how serious I am. You need to clear your schedule for a few days. I want to take you somewhere next weekend. We need a fresh start and some alone time," Leo said making her smile. He knew that she was back on board once he said that. Keller was a hopeless romantic and she lived for spontaneous gestures of love. He didn't really have anything planned, but it wouldn't be hard to put something together. It was the little things that made her smile.

"Where do you want to go?" Keller asked.

"I don't know. We'll discuss that later when I pick you up. Go handle your business and hit me up when you get some free time," Leo said as he kissed her cheek and watched her walk away. He knew without a doubt that Keller was the best woman that he'd ever had, but he still didn't do right by her. She was beautiful and independent and Leo felt intimidated by that at times. He didn't want to lose her, so he tried putting fear in her to keep her around. It seemed to be pushing her away instead, so he had to do better. Keller was the only woman that he'd ever loved, but that didn't keep him from being with others. It was only for sex, but that still was no excuse.

"You ready Mo?" Keller asked her mother when she walked back into the shop. She was in a much better mood since she talked with Leo, but Mo was still feeling some kind of way.

"Sit down and eat the breakfast that I got for you. We need to discuss a few things," Mo replied.

"Okay," Keller said as she did what her mother told her to do. Mo sat patiently and waited until she warmed up her food and took a seat behind her work station.

"Have I ever raised a hand to you or your sister Keller?" Mo calmly asked her daughter.

"No ma'am," Keller replied respectfully.

"Have I ever raised my voice to get my point across to y'all?" Mo inquired.

"No ma'am," Keller repeated truthfully.

Mo was the best mother that they could have asked for, but she never yelled or raised a hand to them. She said something one time and her girls knew to obey her command. Mo was small in stature, but her mere presence commanded respect. She grew up selling drugs and running the streets right along with their father until the day he died. Everybody knew and loved her as well as her brothers. It was crazy because she was so meek and mild. No one would have ever known some of the things that she had done or was capable of doing. As hood as Mo was, she was successful at shielding her girls from the street life and encouraged them to go to school instead. Kia and Keller were naïve to a lot of things, which made it easy for the men in their lives to have the upper hand. Some days Mo regretted not teaching them the basic street knowledge, but it was too late since they were both grown women now.

"Okay, so help me understand how you let a nigga do something to you that I've never done? And don't give me that bullshit lie about him never hitting you. That nigga got you shook, so I already know what's up," Mo said bringing their conversation back to the present.

"It only happened once," Keller said as she lowered her head.

"I'm right here Keller. Your eyes should be on mine when you talk to me," Mo replied.

"Yes ma'am," Keller said as she looked Mo in her eyes.

"I get it, you love him, so I expect you to lie. What I don't expect is for you to be a nigga's punching bag or his doormat. I didn't raise you and Kia to be weak behind no nigga. You better get your mind right and act like you got some sense. Don't be the reason that Pat be burying her son," Mo warned her.

"Yes ma'am," Keller replied once she finished eating her food.

"Alright, now show me this new design that you want me to try on my nails," Mo smiled while changing the subject to a more pleasant one.

"Okay, I hope you like it," Keller said smiling back at her.

She was happy that Mo had decided to talk about something else. She didn't want the entire conversation to be focused on Leo and their shaky relationship. He promised Keller that he was going to do better and she believed him. She needed something good to happen just so Mo and Kia could get off of her back. She just prayed that Leo didn't make a fool out of her again.

Chapter 7

"Who the hell is she anyway? That bitch must be crazy," Brooklyn said as she sat on her sofa and fed her baby.

Brooklyn was Jaden's only sister and she and Kia were close. Jaylynn loved to be at her auntie's house because she got to play with her little cousins DJ and Dominique. Brooklyn and her husband Dominic had just welcomed their third child and second son into the world almost three weeks ago. Since she was still healing from child birth, Kia made it her business to go over to her sister-in-law's house in the afternoons when she got off from work.

"That hoe is very crazy. Her name is Tori, but I call her tore up," Kia said referring to the girl that Jaden use to deal with.

"And what does my brother have to say about her following you and shit?" Brooklyn asked.

"There's nothing that he can say. He's confronted her a million times, but she's not right in the head. He swears that he's not messing with her no more, but I don't believe that. I can't see her acting like that behind a nigga who don't want her no more."

"Girl you'll be surprised. I've seen my fair share of crazy bitches to last me a lifetime. You need to report her ass to the police and get some paperwork on file. That way you can blow her retarded ass away if she comes close to you again," Brooklyn encouraged.

"I never even thought about that, but that's a good idea," Kia acknowledged.

"Either that or put Mo on her ass," Brooklyn laughed.

"She's crazy as fuck, but I wouldn't even do her like that. Mo would probably kill her. But seriously Brook, this is the final straw with me and Jaden. I'm tired of all this breaking up to make up every week. And I'm sick of fighting bitches behind a man that's supposed to belong to me. This shit is getting old and I'm drained. My daughter is getting older and she's seeing too much going on between us," Kia said seriously.

"I understand Kia. I want you and my brother to be together, but you gotta do what's best for you and Jaylynn. She's at the age where she knows and understands what's happening. She loves her daddy, but there's no telling what kind of affect this is having on her."

"The part that hurts me is that my baby thinks this shit is normal. She'll ask me if her daddy still lives with us or did I put him out again. How am I supposed to explain our dysfunctional relationship to a ten year old?" Kia questioned, but her sister-in-law had no answers.

"I don't even know Kia. Dominic and I didn't have the best relationship in the beginning, but I'm happy that we're all good now. You have to show Jaden that you're not playing with his ass. Let him know that you can do the same thing that he does if you choose too."

"Girl your brother is crazy. He's the only man that I've ever been with and he's determined to keep it that way. Well, he's the only man that I've ever had sex with that is," Kia corrected. It was no secret to Jaden and nobody else who knew her that she loved oral sex like a fat kid loved cake. She never had sex with anyone else, but she had no problem letting another man taste her cookies. Jaden got wind of it a few times and it never turned out good.

"But how is that fair to you though Kia? As soon as y'all break up he go lay up in between another bitch's legs, but he be trying to kill a nigga just for flirting with you. You and Keller are some bad bitches and him and Leo better recognize that shit," Brooklyn replied.

Keller and Kia were often mistaken for twins with their almost identical features. Kia was a shade darker than her sister, but the similarities were much the same. Keller was a little thicker than Kia, but they both got their nice shape and petite frame right from Mo.

"It's not fair. I could have been had me a doctor or something from my job. Lord knows they flirt with me all day. One of the surgical techs has been asking me to go out with him for months. I keep turning him down because I'm worried about Jaden's crazy ass," Kia said.

Kia was a medical records coding technician at University Hospital and she turned heads every time she walked through the doors. Because she was so in love with Jaden, Kia never even took any of their advances seriously. They had one surgical tech who she ate lunch with from time to time, but that wasn't about nothing. A little harmless flirting back and forth was as far as it went. He knew about Jaden, but he wasn't intimidated by him.

"Show his ass better than you can tell him. Jaden is in love with you, but he's a typical nigga. They want you to be loyal while they fuck everything in sight," Brooklyn said bringing Kia back to their present conversation.

"I agree Brook, but you see how that turned out last time," Kia said somberly.

She tried moving on from Jaden once before, but that ended in disaster. Kia started dating someone that she went to high school with when she and Jaden broke up once. Things were going good for about a month until Jaden found out about it.

"Yeah, but you can't let that stop you from doing you. Jaden is a selfish bastard with his crazy ass," Brooklyn fussed.

"He is selfish, but he better get his shit together, and quick. I swear I don't get it Brook. Jaden claims that I'm what he wants, but he continually messes around with other females. If he's not happy then he needs to just let me go and be with somebody else."

"That'll never happen. Jaden loves you to death, so I don't get it either. He'll die if he's not with you, but he keeps doing shit to push you away," Brooklyn said as she put Dorian across her shoulder to burp him.

"I want something like what you and Dominic have. Just me and my man and our daughter. Is that too much to ask for?" Kia questioned aloud.

"Be careful what you ask for. This shit wasn't no walk in the park in the beginning either. I had to show his ass that I could move on without him at one time too. Sometimes you have to let them see what they'll be missing," Brooklyn replied.

"I guess," Kia sighed. "Let me grab my baby and head on home."

"Now you do know that it's about to be a fight don't you?" Brooklyn laughed.

"I already know," Kia replied as she yelled for Jaylynn to come inside.

She was out back with Dominic and his kids playing on the swing set. It was always the same thing when she went to Brooklyn or Bryce and Taylor's houses because her daughter never wanted to leave. That was exactly why they both let Jaylynn keep extra clothes and other personal items at their houses. Once she got there it was like pulling teeth to get her to leave.

"You might as well go on home. You got my girl out there about to cry," Dominic said as he walked into the house and took his son from Brooklyn.

"I'm not about to play with that lil girl today. Y'all can have her. Let me just go tell her that I'm leaving," Kia said while making her way to the back yard.

Once she kissed her daughter, Brooklyn walked her out to her car. Kia had barely pulled out of the circular driveway before her phone rang displaying her sister's number.

"Hey girl," Kia said answering the phone on her car's blue tooth.

"Hey my beautiful sister. What are you doing?" Keller asked her.

"Awe shit. What do you want Keller?" Kia questioned.

"Why do you think I want something just because I called you beautiful? We look just alike so you are beautiful," Keller said laying it on thick.

"Bitch you don't have to tell me what I already know. So again, what is it that you want?" Kia repeated.

"Food," Keller replied with one word.

"From where?"

"It doesn't matter. It's homecoming at most of these schools and I've been packed all day," Keller replied.

"Okay. Is Jaden still there? He might be hungry too," Kia said.

"Yeah, he's still here and I'm sure he is. He's been just as busy," Keller replied.

"Alright sis, I'll be there in a few," Kia promised before disconnecting the call.

Since both Jaden and her sister loved Popeye's, she decided to stop there and grab them both something to eat. It was almost seven that evening, so she was happy that she wouldn't have to cook. Jaden would be full when he got home and Jaylynn was staying the night out. Kia was ready to get into her Jacuzzi styled tub and relax with a cold glass of wine.

***

"I ain't fucking with you no more Jaden," Serena said as she stood outside of the barber shop talking to one of her ex-flings.

"Why not?" Jaden questioned as he looked her body over lustfully.

Jaden stood at over six feet tall with a caramel complexion and sexy bedroom eyes. To Serena, he looked like and older thugged out version of the rapper Bow Wow. His arms and chest were covered in tattoos and his 'I don't give a fuck' attitude made her and many other women weak in the knees. The only problem with that was Jaden's love for the mother of his child. He made it known that Kia came first and he didn't care how anyone felt about it.

"What you mean why not? I lost count of how many times you showed up at my house when you and your girl got into it and I never once turned you around. Your ass was in my bed damn near more than I was, but you couldn't even give me two hundred dollars to keep my lights on when I needed you," Serena ranted.

"Man, I told you I didn't have it," Jaden said making her look at him sideways.

Not only was Jaden a successful barber, but he supplied damn near the entire hood with weed and pills. Not many people knew that, but Serena was the one who made most of the deliveries for him. He paid her for doing it, but she had kids and bills, sometimes she still fell short and needed help.

"That's bullshit Jaden. You claimed to not have any money, but Kia drove up two days later in a brand new Benz truck," Serena replied.

"Competing against Kia is the quickest way for you to lose the game," Jaden said as he puffed on the blunt that he walked outside to smoke.

Serena had just dropped off a package for him and came to collect her money. Of course Jaden propositioned her for sex just like he always did, but she wasn't trying to hear him.

"Nobody is trying to compete against her," Serena frowned.

"Please don't. I promise you that it's a waste of your time," Jaden said honestly.

"Whatever Jaden. I already know that Kia got you wrapped around her finger. That's why I don't understand why you still be trying to mess around," Serena replied.

Jaden was about to reply until he spotted Kia getting out of her car that she parked right next to his. He saw the frown on her face as soon as he looked her way. He already knew that he was about to get cussed out and he was prepared for it. Kia was spoiled and she knew that she could get away with talking to him any way she wanted to. She was the only female, besides his mother and sister who could. Kia was heated, so there was no telling what she was going to say. He made it clear that he didn't want her talking to any other men, but he was caught in plain sight talking to another female.

"What's up baby?" Jaden said as he tried to kiss Kia when she walked up to him.

"Put that shit out, it stinks," Kia fussed while turning away from his lips.

"Oh, my bad," Jaden said while smashing his blunt into the concrete wall behind him.

Serena stood there speechless as she watched Jaden obey Kia's commands like he wasn't a grown ass man. Jaden had a slick ass mouth and crazy was a compliment compared to how he behaved most of the time. He had a Tasmanian devil tattooed on his arm and that was a very accurate description of him if she had to say so herself.

"Why is she still standing here?" Kia said pointing to Serena.

"Bye Serena," Jaden said never taking his eyes off of Kia's.

"Wow," Serena said as she walked away and went back to her car. Jaden was just begging her for some ass, but it was a different story once Kia walked up. She knew better then to test Jaden so she left without any problems.

"You go ballistic if you see me talking to one of my male co-workers, but you out here choppin' it up with another bitch like it's cool. Nigga you can play with me if you want to. Your ass gon' be right back by your mama and daddy," Kia threatened as she mushed his head and tried to walk away.

She was the only female that had ever handled Jaden the way that she did. If it were anybody else he wouldn't have hesitated to knock them the fuck out with no remorse.

"Man, calm down. That girl made a drop off for me and that was it," Jaden swore.

"Whatever Jaden. I thought you were done with all of that shit or was that another one of your lies," Kia yelled.

"I told you that I'm trying to get us a house. That's what you told me you wanted."

"That was three years ago Jaden. I'm sure you've saved up enough money to buy two or three houses by now. Being greedy is what's gonna get you caught up."

"I'm not trying to have this conversation with you right now Kia. What are you doing here and where is my baby?" Jaden asked.

"Your daughter is at Brooklyn's house for the night. And I came here to bring you and Keller something to eat," Kia replied.

"That's what's up. A nigga is starving right now," Jaden said rubbing his toned stomach.

"Well, you should have thought about that before I walked up on you talking to another bitch," Kia said as she opened the box of chicken that she'd purchased for him and dumped it all on the sidewalk.

"What the fuck Kia?" Jaden yelled as he watched his meal hit the concrete.

"Fuck you nigga. Let that hoe feed your dog ass," Kia replied as she stepped over her mess and walked into the shop.

Jaden only shook his head and watched her walk away. Kia was a piece of work, but Jaden had made her that way. He'd cheated on her so much that she was insecure about every little thing that he did. He loved Kia to death, but he had to do better. He didn't want to push her away, but he knew that it would happen eventually. The problem with Kia was that she made threats, but she never followed through with any of them. She would put Jaden out for a month or two and then he would be right back like nothing ever happened. If he thought that Kia would really leave him alone for good, he would have calmed down a long time ago. The fact that he knew that she wasn't going anywhere made him keep doing what he was doing. It got so bad that he started leaving half of his clothes at his parents' house just so he wouldn't have to keep bringing them back and forth.

"Come here girl," Jaden said as he grabbed Kia when she walked back outside a few minutes later.

"Fuck you nigga. Keep doing you. Just don't get mad when I do me," Kia said as she continued to walk off.

She was dead ass serious and she was about to show him that two could play the same game. Too many men were trying to get at her, but she was too busy being faithful to his dog ass.

"You see how doing you turned out the last time, huh?" Jaden quizzed with a serious look on his face.

Once when he and Kia separated she started dating a dude named Paul that she knew from high school. Jaden was furious when he found out and he ended up confronting the other man one night. Things quickly went left after Paul told Jaden that he had no intentions of leaving Kia alone. They never even had sex and the nigga was acting like he was sprung. What started out as a normal confrontation ended up with Paul taking a trip to the city morgue. He and Jaden got into a fight and Paul felt played that he didn't win. He threatened Jaden's life, but his life was the one that ended that very same night. Jaden got arrested, but thanks to Kia the charges were dropped a few months later. She swore to the detectives that Jaden was with her the entire night even though he wasn't. She even produced tickets to an outdoors concert that she and Keller went to and said that she went with Jaden instead. Since they didn't have any solid proof and he had a damn good lawyer and alibi, they had to let him walk. That was one of the reasons why he loved Kia so much. She had his back when nobody else did.

"Why you always gotta bring that up every time I talk about moving on?" Kia said with tears in her eyes.

"Why you always gotta try me?" Jaden countered. "Moving on is not an option for either one of us."

"Miss me with the bullshit Jaden. You move on every time we break up and sometimes when we're still together."

"I think you're happier when the crazy Jaden shows up. You act like you hate it when I'm calm. You must want a nigga to act a fool on you like I did back in the day. I'm getting too old for all that shit Kia."

"You're getting too old to be cheating too, but you don't let that stop you," Kia sassed.

"What the fuck am I doing? I'm home with you and my daughter at a decent hour every night. If I'm not with my brothers or cousin, I'm with Dominic and David. You and Jay get all of my time. I stopped clubbing every weekend like you wanted me to and you're still not satisfied," he replied.

"Your brothers, Dominic and David are not the problem. It's your dog ass cousin that I have a problem with. Shawn is a hoe and you become one when you hang with him."

"So what, you want me to stop hanging with my cousin now? If it'll keep down the confusion between us then I'll do it."

"That's not what I'm saying Jaden," Kia started before he cut her off.

"Then what the fuck do you want from me Kia?" He yelled in frustration.

"Stop fucking screaming at me Jaden. Your cousin is not the real issue here, you are. I know you and your ass is sneaky, just like I walked down on you talking to ole girl a minute ago. You can't pay me to believe that it was all about business."

"I keep telling you that I'm not on that shit no more man. We've been straight for almost six months now. Don't start trippin' on me for nothing," he begged.

"We've been straight because you're getting better at doing your dirt. But you're right. I won't trip until you give me something to trip about," Kia promised.

"Just give a nigga credit for trying. That's all I'm asking."

"Okay," Kia agreed.

"I got three more heads to cut and I'm coming straight home. Give me a kiss," Jaden demanded.

He didn't wait for Kia to come to him before he pulled her into his embrace and tongued her down. Bryce pulled up and shook his head when he saw his little brother and his girlfriend outside kissing. He swore that Jaden and Kia had the most dysfunctional relationship that he'd ever seen before in his life. Jaden was head over heels in love, but he couldn't stay faithful to save his life.

"What's up Bonnie and Clyde?" Bryce joked when he walked up. "You done for the day Jaden?"

"Nah, I got like three niggas waiting for me right now," he replied as his phone started ringing.

Kia looked down at the screen at the same time as he did. Although Tori's number wasn't saved, she called so much that they both knew her number just by looking at it.

"But I'm trippin' though," Kia snapped as she pulled away from him and stormed off to her car.

"Fuck!" Jaden yelled as he watched Kia speed away from the shop. He pulled his keys out of his monogrammed barber's smock and prepared to go after her.

"The fuck you going bruh? Didn't you just say that you have three people waiting to get their hair cut," Bryce said.

"Man, fuck them niggas. Tell Brian to handle it," Jaden snapped angrily.

Bryce watched as Jaden hopped into his car and sped out of the parking lot right behind Kia. He swore that if Jaden wasn't his little brother he would have kicked him out of his shop a long time ago.

"What!" Jaden yelled into his phone when he finally answered for Tori. He was on his way home and she had called him over five times.

"Damn, what you doing all that for? I was just calling to put some money in your pockets," Tori said like she was offended.

"Didn't I tell your slow ass not to call my phone no more unless I called you first?" Jaden yelled.

"I'm sorry, but somebody was asking to buy some pills," Tori replied.

"What the fuck you call me for? Call Serena to handle that."

"I did, but she didn't answer. I just didn't want you to miss out on any money."

"Man, fuck that sale! Kia was standing right there when you called. Now I gotta go home and hear this bullshit all night."

"Fuck Kia with her ole insecure ass. She shouldn't have a problem with what you're doing since she's the one benefiting off of the money you're making," Tori yelled.

"You go a lot of mouth over the phone, huh? Be ready to pull my foot out of your ass when I see you. Stupid bitch," Jaden fumed before hanging up in her face.

Chapter 8

"Ahhh!" Tori screamed in frustration as she threw her phone across the room.

She balled up in the middle of her bed and let the tears that she'd been holding in all day finally fall freely. She hated that no matter how nice she tried to be to Jaden, he always shitted on her for Kia. That bitch wasn't the one who was risking her life and freedom going back and forth out of town to pick up drugs for his ass. She wasn't the one who fucked and sucked different men just to get him what he needed when he was running low on product. Kia reaped all the benefits, but Tori put in all the hard work. And it didn't help that she was who Jaden always ran to whenever Kia put him out of a house that he paid the rent on. He stayed some nights at his parents' house, but Tori got her time in with him too. She knew that he fucked Serena a few times, but she wasn't a threat. It was Kia who she wanted out of the picture, but Jaden was in love with that hoe. Tori had gone as far as calling her and telling her personally that she was fucking her man. Jaden tried to kill her after that, but she didn't care. She followed Kia from work a few times and he got his cousin and some of her girls to jump her, so she never did that again. Once Tori found out that she was pregnant, she was excited, but that didn't last very long either. She woke up one morning in excruciating pain and ended up having a miscarriage soon after. It didn't matter anyway since Jaden denied being the father. He made sure he used protection every time they had sex, but when he was drunk he really didn't care. Condoms were the furthest thing from his mind when he was full of that liquor. He didn't even come to see her after she lost their baby. Then he made things worse when he took Kia and their daughter to Hawaii two weeks later. Tori knew that he only did that because his conscience was eating him up.

"What the hell is wrong with you?" Tori's sister Toni asked when she entered the bedroom.

"Nothing," Tori mumbled while drying her tears.

"I hope you ain't crying over Jaden's ass again. You need to let him be and move on," Toni said sternly.

"If it was that easy I would have done that a long time ago. Just stay out of my business," Tori snapped.

"Bitch don't get mad with me because you're in love with a man who's in love with somebody else. I keep telling you that Jaden be using you to do his dirty work. I bet you he wouldn't ask Kia to pick up his dope and sell it for him. That nigga don't even get his own hands dirty. He come through and dick you down every now and then just to keep you happy," Toni replied.

"It's not even like that Toni. I just feel like he's sending me mixed messages. One minute he's spending the night out with me like we're going to be together and then he's telling me not to call him the next. I just want him to keep it real with me and stop telling me what he thinks I want to hear," Tori cried.

"Stop listening to what he's saying and watch his actions. You don't even have a car, but Kia is driving around in a top of the line truck. You live with me and my kids in a small ass three bedroom apartment, but he's trying to buy her a house. His actions are showing you just how he feels. He don't give a damn about you and none of them other hoes. It's all about Kia."

"He rents cars for me when I need him to," Tori said taking his side.

"Yeah, so you can go out of town to pick up his dope. Has he ever rented you a car when you didn't have to make a pick-up or drop-off for him?" Toni asked her naïve little sister.

"I've never asked him to," Tori replied feeling more stupid than she did before.

Her sister was pointing out everything that she already knew, but didn't want to admit.

"You sound stupid. That nigga don't have no love for you. Not even in the bedroom from what you tell me," her sister said before walking out of the room.

She regretted telling her older sister some of the things that went on with her and Jaden in the bedroom. He was more disrespectful there than he was anywhere else. There was nothing gentle about him, but Tori still loved him unconditionally. She wished she didn't, but she couldn't help it. After listening to some of the things that her sister had just said, Tori felt like a damn fool. She didn't want to believe that Jaden didn't care about her, but his actions said otherwise. It was time for Tori to give him an ultimatum. She knew that he would never leave Kia, but she needed him to treat her better than he'd been doing. Either that or he could find another fool to do his dirty work for him. Getting up from the bed, Tori picked up and phone and decided to call her cousin Anaya. She needed to get out of the house and she was hoping that Naya would pick her up.

"Hey girl," Anaya said when she answered the phone.

"What are you getting into tonight?" Tori asked her.

"Probably nothing. I'm so broke I can't even afford to put gas in my damn truck," Anaya complained.

"Broke? Where your man at? Tigga got enough money to stop world hunger and you don't have gas money?" Tori questioned.

"Fuck Tigga! He thinks because he pays all the bills and takes care of the girls that everything is all good. He don't give me any money at all," her cousin revealed.

"Don't you have a debit card or something? Go to the bank and get you some cash."

"His stupid ass took me off of the accounts. He said that I'm always withdrawing and never depositing anything. I've been trying to find me a job just to keep some money in my pockets," Anaya replied.

"That's fucked up. What about Rich? That nigga don't be trying you help you out? He should as much as y'all sneak around with each other."

"Girl please. That lil money that he dish out ain't nothing to get excited over. Once I get my hair and nails done that be gone."

"Tigga is wrong for that shit. I don't know why you just don't leave his ass alone. It don't seem like he wants the relationship no more anyway," Tori said like she had room to talk.

"I don't care what he wants. I ain't going back to that trailer park so he better get over it. That nigga ain't going nowhere as long as I got his daughters. We're a package deal. It's all of us or none of us," Anaya replied.

"Now why you wanna use that man's kids against him like that?" Tori questioned.

"Bitch that's my leverage. I can keep that nigga in check as long as I got his babies. He loves his daughters to death."

"Oh well, that ain't none of my business. I was just calling to see if you wanted to get into something tonight. I'll give you some gas money and pay your way wherever we go."

"That sounds good, but I have to see if Tigga has plans or not. I might have to find me a babysitter."

"Okay. Just call and let me know. Don't take too long or I'll be calling somebody else. I need to get a few drinks in my system," Tori replied.

"You are too pretty to drink as much as you do. Your mystery man is turning you into a straight up alcoholic," Tori scolded.

Tori's mother and Anaya's mother were first cousins, but they weren't very close. Their kids all hung out because they were all around the same age. Anaya's mother was a no nonsense woman when it came to the men in her life, but Tori's mother, Darlene, was the exact opposite. She fell in love fast and didn't know how to let go. A trait that Tori and her sister Toni had unfortunately picked up as well. Tori and Toni were both pretty cinnamon colored girls with shoulder length hair and deep dimples. Toni had gained weight from having four babies, but Tori was still slender with long pretty legs. Anaya thought they were beautiful, but they couldn't see it for themselves. Just like their mother, when they got a man they did everything in their power to keep him. That was exactly how Toni ended up with four kids by four different men. They were good about giving each other advice, but they never took their own. Toni seemed to have gotten better, but according to her, Tori hadn't.

"I just got a lecture from Toni. I don't need one from you too," Tori snapped bringing Anaya back to their conversation.

"Ain't no lecturing over here boo. But I'll call you later and let you know if I can go or not," Anaya said before she hung up. She really wanted to go out with her cousin, but she wasn't in the mood to deal with Tigga's constant attitude. He didn't even try to hide the fact that he wanted out of their relationship. That was the part that hurt her feelings the most.

Chapter 9

"Damn man," Tigga sighed while running his hand through his hair. "When did that nigga get locked up?"

"It's been almost a week now," the man on the other end of the phone replied.

"Man, I need my damn hair cut like right now. My shit is getting too high," Tigga complained.

"Come through and let somebody else get you right."

"Hell nah. Nigga you know I don't play behind my fades. I might have to knock one of them niggas out if they fuck me up. That nigga Jake can't stay out of jail for nothing."

"You already know how he is. But I'll tell that nigga to hit you up whenever he touch down. But the offer still stands if you want to come through to see somebody else."

"I'm waiting on a few contracts that I need to sign, but I might come through when I get out of here," Tigga said before he hung up the phone.

He was in desperate need of a haircut, but his barber was at his home away from home once again. Jake was a fool with the clippers, but he was always into some other shit. Tigga had been going to him for over five years and he trusted him to get him right. He hated to admit it, but it was time for him to find another barber who didn't have so much drama in his life.

"Mr. Coleman, your appointment is here," Tigga's secretary Maria buzzed in pulling him away from his thoughts.

"Tyler, Ms. Maria. Call me Tyler. My grandpa ain't here no more. What you look like calling me Mr. and you're older than me?" Tigga laughed.

"I'm sorry honey. I'll get it together eventually," Maria said.

Maria had worked for his grandfather for years, but she left when her husband took sick. When her husband passed away a year ago, Tigga hired her back with no questions asked. She was good at what she did and she knew the business like it was her own.

"It's okay, but you can send my appointment back here and call it a night. This is it for the day," Tigga informed her.

"Okay, he's on the way back. I'll see you Monday. Have a good weekend," Maria replied.

Tigga shut down his computer and prepared to leave once he handled his last bit of business. He needed to get his hair cut and get home to his girls. Anaya wanted them all to do something for the weekend, but Tigga wasn't really feeling it. Most times they did things with the girls separately if they weren't at home and he was cool with that.

"What the business is?" Dominic spoke when he walked into Tigga's office.

"Same shit, different day," Tigga replied as he stood up and gave him dap.

Dominic and his brother David owned a trucking company that Tigga used to transport materials to different jobs from time to time. He'd been using them for two years and had gotten close with the two brothers since then. They were both married with kids, but they still hung out from time to time.

"Check out the numbers and make sure that everything is in order with what we discussed," Dominic said handing him some contracts to look over.

Tigga scanned over the numbers and nodded his head in agreement before he signed. Dominic added his signature to the papers and gave him a copy of them all.

"What you and David getting into this weekend?" Tigga asked him.

"I'm not doing shit. My wife just had her six week checkup and she's ready to get out of the house. I'm on daddy duty all weekend," Dominic chuckled.

"Damn, lil man is six weeks old already? That time passed fast."

"Yeah, that nigga getting fat as hell too. What you got going on?" Dominic asked.

"Man, I'm trying to get my hair cut, but my barber got locked up. I'm mad as hell that I have to go to somebody new," Tigga complained.

"I got two brother-in-law's that cut hair. They cut me, David and my son's hair," Dominic replied.

"Are they really good? Don't send me there just because that's your people."

"Man I'm telling you, them niggas can cut. I wouldn't let them touch me and my son's head if they couldn't. I don't give a damn if they are family."

"That's what's up. Where they cut at?" Tigga asked him.

Dominic reached into his wallet and pulled out two cards. One had Brian's information on it and the other had Jaden's.

"Let me call and see if they got a crowd in there," Dominic offered as he pulled out his phone and dialed a number.

He talked on the phone for a few seconds before he turned his attention back to Tigga.

"So-Xclusive? I've heard of them before," Tigga said as he read the card trying to figure out where he'd heard the name before.

"My brother-in-law Bryce owns the shop and he does tattoos upstairs. They do hair and nail and shit downstairs," Dominic replied.

"Yeah, I went there with Anaya a while back to get her a tattoo. I didn't know that was your people."

"Yeah, three of my wife's brothers and her two cousins work there. Jaden said he's free for another hour so he can hook you up right quick," Dominic informed him.

"That's what's up. I'm on my way over there as soon as I lock up. That might be my new spot if everything works out," Tigga replied.

He locked up his office and followed Dominic down the hall. Once he set the alarm and locked up the building, he got into his truck and headed to the barber shop.

***

"No Leo, I'm sick of this shit. You swore that things were going to be different, but it's the same shit. This bitch has been playing on my phone for over two weeks," Keller yelled into the phone.

"That shit ain't my fault. I don't know why she's playing on your phone. I don't even know that girl like that," he swore.

"Why don't you just stop lying for once in your life? That bitch knows too much about me. How did she know that we went out of town last weekend?" Keller asked him.

"I don't know. She's friends with my sister. Maybe she told her."

"That's bullshit! So you don't know her like that, huh? At first you claimed that you didn't know who she was at all. Now you're saying that she's friends with your sister. You're messing around with that hoe. I can't see her playing on my phone and shit for nothing. If you want her then leave me alone and go be with her. I'm not making you stay with me," Keller yelled.

She was standing outside of the shop having yet another argument with her no good ass man. The same girl that Leo claimed to not know was blowing her phone up yet again. It was no coincidence that she seemed to call every time he left the house to go handle business. More than likely he was calling her as soon as he was away from Keller. There was no other way to explain the perfect timing of her calls.

"If I wanted the bitch I could have had her a long time ago. And you better watch how the fuck you talk to me. I'll come to that shop and knock your stupid ass out," Leo threatened.

"You ain't gon' do shit!" Keller yelled feeling confident because he wasn't near her. Besides, Jaden was in the shop and Leo knew better than that.

"Keep talking that hot shit. You gotta come home eventually."

"Wait on it. Go spend time with your other bitch because this one is done. I'll be there to get my shit this weekend. I'm moving in with my sister," Keller said even though she didn't mean it.

"Don't play with me Keller. You better have your ass home when I get there. Try me if you want to."

"Fuck you!" Keller yelled right before she hung up in his face.

"Damn. I'm happy that wasn't me on the other end of your line," Tigga joked when he walked up.

Keller turned around and smiled at him. The butterflies in her stomach started dancing to the beat as soon as their eyes connected. Tigga was fine as hell even without his usual tight fade that he always sported. His hair had grown higher than she'd ever seen it, but he was still sexy. She and Tigga flirted via text message all the time, but she was still kind of nervous whenever they were face to face.

"I'm sorry that you had to hear that, but you know that I would never talk to you like that," Keller replied.

"I would never give you a reason to," he winked making her blush.

"What are you doing around this way?" She asked him.

"My boy hooked me up with one of the barber's here. The other nigga who used to cut me up went to jail. What you doing around here?" He asked her.

"I work here. I'm the nail tech and make-up artist. What barber did he refer you to?"

"His name is Jaden. You know him?" Tigga asked.

"Yeah, that's my brother-in-law," she smiled.

"How is that possible when my boy said that Jaden is his brother-in-law? Do you know Dominic?" He questioned.

"Yeah, his wife Brooklyn is Jaden's sister. Jaden is my sister Kia's boyfriend. They have a daughter together," Keller replied.

"Damn, y'all like one big happy family over here. I forgot that Tessa told me that you do her nails. I never knew where you worked at though."

"Well, now you know just in case you wanna feed me one day," Keller joked.

"Or maybe I might want you to feed me one day, but not food," Tigga flirted making her weak in the knees.

"Are you always this straight forward with everybody?" Keller asked him.

"I try to be," Tigga shrugged. "Come inside and show me who Jaden is."

Keller grabbed his hand and walked him through the front door. The shop was fairly empty for a Friday, but Co-Co and Candace both had customers. Brian was finishing up with a cut and Jaden was sitting down in his chair playing on his phone. He looked at Keller strange when he saw her walk through the door holding an unknown man's hand.

"Yes Keller bitch. Now that's the kind of man that you need on your arm. Leo's ole Welvin looking ass needs to go," Co-Co said making his sister laugh.

"Damn Co-Co, not Welvin," Candace laughed.

"Bitch Welvin actually looks better," he replied.

"Shut up Co-Co," Keller yelled. "Jaden this is Tigga, the one Dominic told you about."

"Oh yeah, what's up?" Jaden said as he stood up and shook Tigga's hand.

They exchanged greetings before Jaden instructed him to have a seat. After Tigga told him how he wanted his hair cut, Jaden draped the cape around his neck and got right to work. Keller was done for the day, so she sat around and talked to everybody else. She was pissed with Leo, so she was catching a ride to Kia's house with Jaden. He thought she was playing, but she was not stepping one foot in their house that night.

"How do you know him?" Candace whispered when she took a seat next to Keller. She'd just finished braiding her client's hair and was waiting for another one to arrive.

"That's Tessa's brother," Keller replied.

"He's cute," Candace complimented.

"And you're married," Keller said.

"Bitch I'm married, but I'm not blind. David probably compliments other women all the time. But what's up with you and him? Y'all looked kind of familiar just a few minutes ago."

"Nothing is up with us. That's my best friend's brother," Keller replied.

"That's the nigga that you be texting all day. The one who be having you smiling like a crazy person," Candace said.

"You and your brother are so nosey," Keller laughed.

"Yeah we are, but I'm right, huh?" Candace asked.

"Yeah, that's him, but don't tell nobody. Leo will go crazy on my ass if that gets back to him," Keller added.

"Leo goes crazy on your ass anyway. It'll just be worse if he finds out," Candace countered.

Keller hated that everyone knew what kind of person that Leo really was. It was crazy because he wasn't like that in the beginning. He was kind of insecure, but he really didn't have a reason to be. He was Keller's second boyfriend and sex partner and she had never cheated on him. Her first boyfriend, Carlos, cheated on her which is how she ended up with Leo in the first place. Keller couldn't help but feel that she'd jumped from the frying pan right into the fire. Carlos might have cheated, but he never raised a hand to her. She left him without a second thought and never looked back. Leo, on the other hand, was a serial cheater who couldn't keep his hands to himself, but she couldn't stay away from him.

"Did you eat yet?" Tigga asked snapping Keller back to reality.

"Um, just some chips and juice. I'll probably grab something when me and Jaden leave here," Keller replied.

"Let's go get something to eat. I'll bring you home," Tigga said reaching his hand out for her to take.

"Awe shit nah. You better go get your meal girl," Co-Co instigated.

"Shut your messy ass up," Jaden replied before Keller could say anything.

"Let me grab my purse," Keller said laughing at Jaden and Co-Co going back and forth.

Tigga talked to Jaden for a few minutes until Keller came from the back of the shop. Once she said a few parting words to everybody, she and Tigga got in his truck and pulled off.

"You like your hair cut?" Keller asked him.

"That nigga is nice with them clippers. That's my new spot. You like it?" Tigga asked.

"I love it," Keller smiled. "I guess that means I'll be seeing you more often."

"Yeah, but you don't have to wait until I come to the shop. You can see me whenever you want to. You got my number."

"And how is that when we both have somebody waiting for us at home?" Keller inquired.

"I don't know about you, but nobody is waiting at home for me but my girls."

"What about Anaya?" Keller questioned.

"What about her?" Tigga shrugged.

"That bad huh?" Keller asked.

"It must not be all that great with you and ole boy either. You wouldn't be with me right now if it was," he pointed out.

Keller turned her head and looked out of the window without replying. She wasn't sure if Tessa had told her brother about her and Leo's crazy relationship, but she prayed that she didn't.

"Don't feel no kind of way baby girl. I'm in some shit that I don't want to be in too. If it wasn't for my daughter's I would have been gone a long time ago," Tigga said making her feel a little better.

"At least you have an excuse for staying. Me and Leo don't even have kids together."

"It's not really an excuse. I just want my girls to know that I'm not a deadbeat ass nigga. If I'm with their mama or not I'm going to take care of them. I just know how Anaya is. If we're not together she won't even let me see my kids. I would hate to get the court system involved, but that's what my mama wants me to do. I probably won't have a choice once I leave her anyway," Tigga replied.

"So you're really gonna leave her?"

"As soon as you leave ole boy and agree to be with me," Tigga smirked.

"Where are we going?" Keller asked changing the subject.

"Wherever you want to go," Tigga said while grabbing her hand.

The butterflies in her stomach started moving about as soon as his hand touched hers. Although she was a little nervous, Keller was happy to be with him.

"Let's go to Katie's and get some oysters," she suggested.

"Alright," Tigga said as if her every wish was his command.

Being with him was much different than being with Leo. He always wanted to call all the shots while Keller followed his lead. Tigga seemed to be the considerate type and she could get use to that. She didn't know where their friendship was going, but she was curious to find out. Leaving Leo and getting with him was sounding better and better even though it would probably never happen.

Chapter 10

"You better stop playing on my fucking girl's phone," Leo yelled to the woman who was on the other end of his line.

He and Keller had been getting into it almost every day for the past few weeks over one thing or another. They were doing fine when they came back from their weekend getaway, but that didn't last very long. Crystal, his occasional fuck buddy and friend of his sister, was on some bullshit. She'd been playing on his and Keller's phones non-stop, causing a strain in their relationship. He and Keller argued and fought just about every single day as a result. Leo was pissed because she started spending more and more time at the shop just to get away from him.

"Fuck your girl nigga. You need to be trying to take care of your son," Crystal yelled snapping him back to reality.

"That ain't my fucking baby and I'm tired of you saying that shit."

"Prove it then. Let's take a blood test," Crystal requested.

"I don't need one. I know that lil boy ain't mine."

"My son looks just like you and your entire family knows it. You're only denying him because you don't want Keller to find out about it. I bet if that bitch got pregnant you would take care of hers."

"You damn right I would. That's my fucking girl," Leo yelled.

"She's your girl, but you stay in between my legs more than my underwear," Crystal replied with a sarcastic chuckle.

"You keep opening up for me so that's all on you. You claim I'm a dead beat who don't take care of his responsibilities, but you keep letting me hit it. You sound real stupid right now."

"Let's see how stupid I sound when I show up to your girl's shop and introduce her to her two year old step-son," Crystal threatened.

"Bitch try me if you want to. Your son gon' be without a mama and a daddy. This is my last time telling you this shit. Stop calling my girl's phone and stop calling mine. That lil boy ain't mine so you better go find his real daddy," Leo yelled.

"Nigga you are his real daddy and I won't stop doing shit until you start acknowledging that. If you're so sure then take a blood test. It's as simple as that," Crystal replied.

"Fuck that blood test and fuck you too," Leo said before he hung up in her face.

He hated to admit it, but he knew that Crystal was right. Her son did look just like him, but he refused to acknowledge him. Crystal was friends with his sister Leandra and that was how he met her. She knew that he had a girlfriend, but she didn't have a problem playing the role of side chick. It started out with them just having casual sex with no strings attached. That was all fine and good until Crystal started catching feelings. Leo tried to back away from her, but then she started claiming to be pregnant. Of course he denied being the father from day one, but she had his entire family convinced otherwise. That was proved when his mother and sister threw her a big baby shower. Leandra swore to Leo that Crystal hadn't been with anyone else since that started messing around, but he wasn't trying to hear it. Keller was his heart and he couldn't lose her behind somebody else claiming to have his baby. It news of the baby somehow managed to get back to Keller anyway, but he still denied having any knowledge of it. The ringing of Leo's phone quickly shook his from his thoughts. He was tempted not to answer when he saw Leandra calling, but he was curious as to what she had to say.

"What?" Leo yelled when he answered the phone.

"You are so wrong for how you're handling the situation Crystal. I know that you don't want her, but you don't have to talk to her like that," Leandra said.

"Mind your business Leandra. I told her stupid ass about playing on my girl's phone, but she keeps taking me to play with."

"The only thing she wants is for you to take care of her son."

"And what that got to do with Keller?" Leo yelled.

"It has nothing to do with Keller. I already told her that she was dead wrong for calling Keller's phone. You and Crystal just need to be adults and put aside y'all differences for your son."

"That ain't my fucking son! I wish y'all stop trying to put that lil boy on me," Leo shouted.

"You need to stop lying to yourself. Leon looks just like you and my son," Leandra replied.

That was another thing that pissed Leo off. Crystal's stupid ass made sure that she named her baby something close to his. He knew that she was doing it just to be messy, but he couldn't do anything about it.

"Maybe she needs to blood test your baby daddy if he looks like your son," Leo laughed.

"My son looks just like your ugly ass nigga," Leandra spat angrily.

"Whatever man, I still say that lil nigga ain't mine."

"Take the test and prove it then," Leandra challenged.

"I'm not doing shit. Just tell that bitch to lose me and my girl's number and we won't have no problems."

"I hope making Keller happy is worth not having a relationship with your only child," his sister spat angrily.

"It is, no doubt about that," Leo said before he hung up in her face.

He hadn't heard from Keller since earlier that morning so he decided to give her a call. When his call went to voicemail, he dialed the shop's number and waited for someone to answer.

"So X-clusive," a male voice said when he answered the phone.

"May I speak to Keller?" Leo asked.

"Aye, is Keller still here?" The man yelled out to someone.

Leo couldn't hear what the other person was saying, but the man came back and repeated it for him.

"Keller ain't here," he said once he was back on the phone.

"You know what time she's coming back?" Leo questioned.

"She's gone for the day," he answered impatiently.

"Alright, cool," Leo said before hanging up the phone.

He tried Keller's line once again, but he still didn't get an answer. Assuming that she was on her way home, Leo sat on the sofa and turned on the TV. He decided to chill out and play his game until she arrived.

***

"Just taste it and see how you like it," Keller said as she tried to shove some food into Tigga's mouth.

"Hell no, I'm not eating no raw fish," Tigga said referring to the sushi that she was trying to feed him.

"It's not raw. It's cooked all the way through. It's like a Po-boy without the bread. Look, its fried shrimp with oysters and fish rolled up together," Keller explained.

"Alright, but if it's nasty I'm spitting it out on your plate," Tigga teased.

He opened his mouth and bit the sushi roll that Keller had put into his mouth. He had to admit that she was right and it tasted better than he thought it would. He was happy when he went to the shop to get his hair cut and ran into her. It was early in the week and that just happened to be one of her slow days. Since they both hadn't eaten he invited her out to an early dinner and she accepted.

"You like it huh?" Keller asked with a huge smile covering her face.

"Yeah, but I like your pretty ass even more," Tigga replied making her blush.

"I like you too, but that's about as far as things with us will probably go," Keller replied.

"How you figure?" Tigga questioned with raised brows.

"We're both in relationships or did you forget that bit of information?"

"No, I'm in a situation that I'm about to get out of. Even though I don't respect it, you're the one that's in a relationship," Tigga informed her.

"You don't respect my relationship?" Keller smirked.

"Fuck no. Any nigga that puts his hands on a female gets no respect from me," Tigga answered making Keller turn her head in embarrassment.

"Stop doing that Keller. You don't have anything to be embarrassed about," Tigga said as he turned her head back to face him.

"I just feel like I be provoking him sometimes. Like right now. I should be at home, but I'm out having dinner with you instead," Keller said shaking her head.

"So you're really gonna sit here and make excuses for why that nigga beat on you?" Tigga asked her as he folded his muscular arms across his chest.

"No, I'm not making excuses. I'm just saying that I know what sets him off and I still do it anyway," Keller replied.

"Keller you're a grown ass woman. That sounds like something that a child would say. I don't give a fuck what you do or don't do, that nigga don't have no business putting his hands on you," Tigga said angrily.

"You're right," Keller nodded in agreement.

"But enough about that clown. I'm trying to spend some time you. I got vacation property in Florida that I always bring my girls to. You need to try to get away and come with us one weekend," Tigga suggested.

"And what about Anaya?" Keller asked.

"What about her? Tessa and my mama always come with us. She can chill with them while I chill with you," Tigga shrugged.

"You are a mess," Keller laughed as she finished her food.

She enjoyed her time with Tigga just like she always did. He made it his business to bring her lunch or just come see her at least two to three times a week. Keller knew that she was falling for him because she found herself looking forward to his visits. Their conversations just seemed to flow effortlessly and she didn't have to watch what she said around him. Leo was always going off about one thing or another and it felt good to not have to deal with that.

"I hate when our time together comes to an end, but I know you have to get home," Tigga said as they walked to his truck.

"I know, but I'll be at Tessa's house this weekend for your mama's birthday dinner," Keller replied.

"Come early so we can chill for a while," he suggested.

"Okay," Keller agreed with a smile.

She sent Tessa a text letting her know that she was on the way to her house. Tigga always dropped her off at his sister's house whenever they spent time together, so that Tessa could bring her home. Once they pulled up, Keller opened the door to get out before Tigga stopped her.

"I want a kiss," Tigga said as he pulled her over to his side.

He didn't give Keller a chance to reject him before he pressed his soft lips against hers. Melting into his embrace, Keller stuck her tongue in his mouth and used it to explore. Tigga's lips were so soft and his tongue felt like velvet in her mouth. Keller almost wet her underwear when Tigga started sucking on her tongue. She didn't want to pull away, but she had to do it. If not she would have been giving in up to Tigga in his truck right in front of Tessa's house.

"Damn," Tigga mumbled. "I wanna see you again tomorrow."

"My work load is kind of light so we can do that," Keller replied.

Tigga got out of his truck and walked her up to Tessa's front door right as Tessa was coming out of it. He gave Keller another small peck on her lips before promising to see her the following day.

"Yes indeed," Tessa drawled once her brother pulled off. "Y'all kissing and shit."

"Girl stop being so dramatic. That lil small peck on the lips ain't nothing."

"Bitch stop lying. I saw y'all out there fogging up the windows in that truck," Tessa laughed.

"Your ass is too nosey," Keller blushed.

"My new sister-in-law," Tessa yelled while pulling her into a tight hug.

"No I'm not either. I have a man at home boo."

"Yeah, for now," Tessa replied as she got into her car and started it up.

She and Keller made small talk until it she pulled up to her apartment complex. Once she made sure that her friend was safely inside, Tessa pulled off and headed home. Keller saw the lamp on in the living room, but she headed straight to her bedroom instead. She really didn't have anything to say to Leo and she was sure that the feelings were mutual. He'd called her at least five times that night and she didn't pick up once. She was having a good time with Tigga and hearing his voice would have probably ruined it for her.

"So you didn't see me calling you all night?" Leo asked when he walked into the bedroom. "Where were you?"

Keller was sure that he'd called the shop and found out that she was gone, so there was no need for her to lie about being at work.

"I was with Tessa," she replied telling only half of the truth.

"You can't answer your phone when you're with Tessa?" He questioned as he walked up on her.

Keller's heart started beating rapidly in her chest because she knew how unpredictable Leo could be.

"I was still mad with you and I didn't want to talk," she replied nervously.

"Or maybe it's because you weren't with Tessa like you said you were," he yelled as he raised his hand and delivered a hard slap to her face. Keller stumbled a little, but she didn't go down to the ground.

"Yes I was," Keller yelled as she grabbed her stinging face.

"Bitch you think I'm stupid. It's after ten o'clock. I called that shop around six this evening and you were already gone for the day. Your lying ass wasn't with Tessa," he fumed as his closed fist came down on her face and busted her nose.

"Noooo! Stop! I'm calling Mo!" Keller screamed as she tried to cover her face. Her nose was burning and the blood was dripping down into her opened mouth. She was trying to fight him back and protect her face at the same time.

"I don't give a fuck. I'll get somebody to bury Mo's ass right next to you," Leo replied angrily. He knew that he was just talking shit, but he was heated at the moment.

"Leave me alone," Keller yelled while still trying to defend herself.

"Ah fuck!" Leo screamed out in pain when Keller bit down hard on his hand.

Keller didn't give him a chance to get right before she kicked him in between his legs as hard as she could.

"Bitch, I'm a kill you," Leo threatened as he went down to the floor howling in pain.

Keller grabbed her keys and purse and ran straight for the front door. She would have hopped in the car, but she didn't know if Leo was behind her or not. There was a gas station on the corner from their house so she ran the short distance until she got there. Thankfully no one was inside when she walked through the doors. She was sure she looked a hot mess with blood on her face and her hair all over her head.

"Are you okay?" One of the workers asked her.

"Where's the bathroom?" Keller inquired.

When he pointed her in the direction, she hurriedly walked away and made her way inside. Just like she'd suspected, she looked like she'd been in a cat fight with a woman instead of a man who was supposed to love her. She grabbed a wad of paper towels and began to clean herself up right as her phone started to ring. She ignored the call when she saw that it was Leo calling and scrolled through her contacts trying to see who she would call. Calling Kia was out of the question because she didn't want to hear her mouth. She would have called Tessa, but she was sure that she would tell her brother what happened. She couldn't call anyone at the shop because Jaden would find out about it then. After searching for a few minutes, Keller decided to call her cousin Rachel. They didn't talk every often, but she knew that she would come and pick her up.

"Hey Keller," Rachel said when she answered the phone.

"Hey cousin. Are you busy right now? I need a huge favor," Keller replied.

"I'm not really busy. I'm just riding around with my boyfriend," Rachel replied.

"I need a ride. Do you think your boyfriend would mind coming to get me?" Keller asked.

"Not at all. Where are you?" Rachel asked.

Keller gave her cousin her location and Rachel assured her that they were on the way. Keller used her free time to get herself together so that she didn't look too messed up. She pulled a comb from her purse and combed her wild hair. After thoroughly washing her face, she put some foundation on to cover whatever marks Leo had left on her face. Thankfully her shirt was black because it was probably covered in blood. After putting some gloss on her lips, Keller looked at her reflection in the mirror. Her nose was a little swollen, but it wasn't very noticeable. She appeared to be the picture of perfection on the outside, but internally it was a different story.

"Are you outside cousin?" Keller asked when she answered the phone for Rachel.

"Yeah, you can come out," Rachel replied.

Keller checked herself out one more time before she finally emerged from the bathroom and made her way out of the front door. She scanned the small parking lot looking for Rachel's car, but she didn't see it anywhere. Keller jumped when a horn blew, but she looked in the direction that it came from.

"I know she didn't send no damn cab for me," Keller spoke aloud to herself.

She was just about to pull out her phone to call Rachel when she jumped out of the cab and yelled for her. Keller walked over to the cab and peeped inside. She was shocked to see the same cab driver who drove her to Kia's house a few months ago sitting behind the wheel.

"Keller, this is my boyfriend Gary," Rachel said introducing the two of them.

"We've already met," Gary chuckled.

"Really? When?" Rachel questioned.

"Remember a few months ago when I told you about the lady who took a picture of my plates and asked me a million questions?" Gary asked.

"That was her?" She laughed while pointing to Keller.

"Shut up Rachel. You know how I feel about cab drivers," Keller said once she got into the back seat of the cab.

"Well enlighten me after you tell me where I'm bringing you," Gary said.

Keller gave him Kia's address right before she told him why she feared cabs and cab drivers. Gary turned out to be cool and she could tell that he really liked her cousin. She ended up sitting in front of Kia's house for over an hour just talking to the two of them. Rachel made her promise to call her more and Keller made her promise not to tell anyone about her needing a ride that night. She was happy that Kia was asleep when she entered the house and Jaden was too high to even pay attention to her. He gave her a pair of Kia's new underwear and some pajamas and she was on her way soon after. Once she took her bath, Keller powered her phone off and went into a deep sleep a few minutes later.

Chapter 11

After showing their identification and signing in, Jaden, his father Bryce, Sr., and his cousin Shawn sat at the table and waited for the inmates to be led into the visitation room. Shawn's father, Shaquille, who was also Bryce's brother and Jaden's uncle, had been locked up for two years of his ten year sentence. He had two hour visits twice a month and he could always count on Jaden to be there for each one. Although Shaquille had six kids of his own, Jaden was always his favorite nephew. They hung out all the time when he was home and their ways were strikingly similar. That was the part that his older brother Bryce hated. Shaquille was always known as the crazy one in the family and Jaden was his young protégé. His other nephews walked a straight line, but Jaden was the rebel. From murder charges to drug cases, he'd gone to jail and beat them all. Unfortunately the same couldn't be said for Shaq. He was serving time on a manslaughter charge, but he was thankful that it wasn't more. They tried to give him second degree murder, but his lawyer got it reduced.

"What's up Shaq?" Jaden beamed when his uncle walked into the room and over to their table. All three men stood up and gave him a hug before they sat back down to talk.

"What's good with you nephew?" Shaq asked Jaden.

"Ain't nothing. Just working and chillin'," Jaden replied.

"And staying out of trouble I hope," his uncle said.

Although he'd influenced a lot of Jaden's bad behavior in the past, he didn't want his favorite nephew to end up where he was.

"He's been alright lately," Bryce spoke up on his son's behalf.

"That's what's up. What about you and Shaquell? Y'all been alright?" Shaq asked his son while also referring to his daughter.

"Yeah, everything is good. Quell is still going to school and I'm still working," Shawn replied.

"That's good. And how's your wife and the rest of the crew?" He asked Bryce.

"Everybody is good. You know I've never had any real problem out of my other kids. As long as this one here is calm then it's all good," Bryce said referring to Jaden.

"That nigga better stay calm. You and Kia still hanging in there, huh?" Shaq asked Jaden.

"You know I ain't going nowhere," Jaden replied.

"I already know. But let's talk after we get us something to eat," Shaq said as she stood to his feet.

The prison had a fully functioning cafeteria with some of the best food that you could ever want. The inmates who ran it cooked better than most women could ever dream of. Bryce and Shawn already knew the routine. They told Jaden what they wanted to eat and he got up and walked away with his uncle to place their orders. Shaq always liked to talk to Jaden alone to see what was really up with him. He knew how his brother was and he didn't like to talk around him.

"You know I don't like to talk in front of Big Bryce, but what's really good with you? You still doing your lil side hustle?" Shaq asked Jaden.

"Yeah man, but I need to find me another runner. Tori is starting to be more trouble than she's worth," Jaden replied.

"That's because you started fucking her. I told you not to go there with her. She's crazy just like her mama. That's why I left her fatal attraction having ass alone," Shaq said.

He had once dated Tori's mother Darlene and that was how Jaden had met Tori.

"Man, she's good at what she does and that's the only reason why she's still around. But that bitch goes too far at times. I had to get Quell and some of her girls to beat her ass a few times. Bitch following Kia home from work and calling all day. I don't need that kind of drama in my home life," Jaden complained.

"You must still be messing with her ass. That's the only reason I can see for her acting like that."

"You already know how I get when I start drinking. Anybody with a pussy can get it," Jaden said making his uncle laugh.

"And her crazy ass probably think it's more to it than just fucking. In her mind y'all are in a relationship."

"That bitch is crazy. I need you to make some calls and find me somebody else. I can't have Kia on my back all the time behind Tori's ole stupid ass. I'm almost where I need to be financially and then I'm pulling out. I just want to buy my girl a nice house and put a big ring on her finger. I'll be good after that," Jaden promised.

"I'm holding you to that too. Kia is a good girl. You can keep playing if you want to. Another nigga gon' step in and take your spot," Shaq warned him.

"I hope a nigga is ready to die behind that pussy too. I wish Kia would play with me with another nigga," Jaden replied meaning every word that he'd just spoken.

"Well, stop giving her a reason," Shaq said giving his nephew something to think about.

Jaden noticed that Kia had been kind of quiet lately. After he followed her home from the shop that one time, they'd been arguing non-stop for days. Maybe she got tired of the back and forth because she'd calmed down and seemed to not care what he did anymore after that. She had Jaden wondering what was going on because that wasn't like her at all. Pushing his thoughts of Kia to the side, Jaden enjoyed the two hour visit with his uncle. His father had three brothers and a sister, but Shaq was always his favorite. That's what scared Bryce, Sr. the most. Jaden reminded him so much of his baby brother until it was scary. What was even scarier was his behavior was almost identical to Shaq's from the moment he entered the world. Bryce and his wife never had to go to school for the rest of their sons, but along came Jaden. He got suspended at least once a month and he feared nothing but the Lord up above. He took risks and he wasn't afraid of the consequence. His mother Pam always questioned where she went wrong with her youngest son, but the answer was never clear. Jaden had his own mind and not even she could change it.

"Shaq looks good," Bryce said when they were on their way back home. The prison was only an hour away so they didn't have far to drive.

"Yeah, he does," Jaden agreed right as his phone started ringing to Jaylynn's ringtone. Without asking his son's permission, Bryce reached over and pressed the talk button on the radio.

"Hey Paw-paw baby," he said once the call was connected.

"Hey Paw-paw," Jaylynn yelled excitedly. "Is my daddy at your house?"

"I'm right here Jay. What's up baby?" Jaden asked his daughter.

"Mama said that she's going somewhere with her work friends tonight and I'm staying with you. Can you bring me to get a new game?" Jaylynn asked.

"I just got you a new game, but I'll get you another one. Put your mama on the phone baby girl," Jaden requested.

"Okay, hold on daddy," Jaylynn said as she yelled for Kia. It sounded like she was running through the house, but Kia got on the phone a short time later.

"Hello," Kia said in her sweet, soft voice.

"What's up with you?" Jaden asked her.

"Nothing. Did Jay tell you what I said?"

"Yeah she did, but I should have heard it from you," Jaden replied.

"Okay, well I'm going out for drinks with Andrea and some of my other co-workers," Kia informed him.

"So what, is this like an every weekend thing now?" Jaden inquired.

"What do you mean?" Kia questioned.

"I mean just what I said. You went out with Andrea last weekend and the weekend before that. You trying to make a habit out of this shit now?"

"How am I making this a habit? I barely go anywhere unless I'm with my sister or you. If you don't want me to go just say so," Kia replied getting angry.

"Nah, it's cool, you can go. I'm about to drop my pops off at home and I'll be there."

"Okay," Kia said before she hung up the phone.

"She on some bullshit," Jaden said as soon as Kia was off the line.

"Don't start your mess boy. The girl only said that she was going out with some friends. What's wrong with that? Your ass used to be in the clubs more than the bartenders," Bryce argued.

"Man, I know Kia. I've been with her ass since she was fifteen years old. She's on some bullshit, but she better be good at covering up her tracks. On God, I'm dealing with her and whatever nigga that she's bold enough to creep with. Bitch act like she's not happy when I'm calm and chillin'. She can unleash the beast if she wants to. Its gon' be hard to put him back in his cage," Jaden warned.

"Boy, I'm telling you right now, I'm not running to no jailhouse to bail your ass out no more. You can get out there and act a fool, but you're on your own Jaden. I'm sick of this shit. You not about to give me and my wife a heart attack behind your bullshit. You almost killed us the last time with all your foolishness."

"Almost doesn't count," Jaden said pissing his father off.

"Stupid muthafucker! You not gon' be satisfied until them people lock your ass up for good. I don't know where we went wrong with you Jaden. I swear I regret the day I started letting you run with Shaq. That nigga rubbed off on you in the worst way. Y'all just better not involve my grandbaby in none of y'all mess. You already got her head messed up with that crazy shit you be talking," Bryce fussed.

Aside from Kia, Jaden's parents were the only ones that talked crazy to him without him reacting to it. He knew not to go too far with his daddy because Bryce, Sr., would pop him in the mouth with no questions asked. He didn't give a damn how grown he was.

"My baby is good. This don't have nothing to do with her," Jaden replied.

"This got everything to do with her when you got her brainwashed with your crazy ass rules. You and Kia got her believing that y'all dysfunctional ass relationship is normal. If a man do that to her you gon' be trying to kill him."

"I ain't gon' try to kill him. A nigga play with Jaylynn and he's as good as dead," Jaden swore.

"Just bring me home bruh. Ain't no getting through to you," his father said giving up his attempt at talking to him.

Jaden shrugged uncaringly and did as he was told. Once he dropped his father and Shawn off, he picked up Jaylynn and took her to get her game. When they made it back home Jaylynn went straight to her room to play her new game while Jaden went to find Kia. She was standing in their walk in closet trying to find something to wear when he entered.

"Where y'all going have drinks at?" Jaden asked her.

"We're going to Cheddar's," she replied.

"So y'all are going all the way to Slidell just to have some drinks?" Jaden questioned skeptically.

Kia wasn't a street chick and it showed just by what she was saying. She wanted Jaden to believe that she was going forty-five minutes away from home just to have drinks with her girls. He smelled the bullshit from a mile away, but he just let her keep digging her grave.

"Yes Jaden. We just try to go somewhere different every time we go out. What's with all the questions?" Kia asked.

"You need some money?" He asked ignoring her question.

"No, I'm good," she replied. "You want me to fix y'all something to eat before I leave?"

"No, Jay wants me to order her a pizza later. Come chill with me before you leave," Jaden requested making Kia smile.

She already knew what that meant and she was down. Chill was his code word for sex, especially when Jaylynn was home. Jaden locked the bedroom door while watching as Kia stripped down out of her tank and shorts. She was in a daze when he started taking off his clothes and she almost wanted to cancel her plans for the evening. Then when she thought about the fun that she would be missing out on she abandoned that idea just as quickly as it came.

"You love me?" Jaden questioned as he looked deep into her eyes.

"Yes," Kia replied nervously as he pushed her back onto their huge bed and climbed in between her legs. It felt like Jaden was trying to read her mind as he continued to stare at her.

"I love you to death. Remember that," he replied as he dipped down lower and buried his face in between her legs.

As much as Kia loved oral sex she was too tense to enjoy Jaden's warm tongue flicking up and down her womanhood. She'd never felt like that before, but she was ready for him to stop.

***

"Daddy I'm so full," Jaylynn said as she and Jaden lounged on the sofa and watched a movie. Kia had been gone for a few hours, so it was just the two of them spending time together.

"I told you not to eat three slices of pizza. Your little body can't handle that much food," Jaden laughed as he rubbed her belly.

"I know, but it was good," Jaylynn replied.

"Jay can we look at something else? We watch this same movie almost every day," Jaden complained. Jaylynn loved the movie Matilda. She had it recorded and wanted him to watch it every time they spent time together.

"But this is my favorite movie. I wish Bailey and Breanna were here. This is their favorite movie too," Jaylynn said speaking of Bryce's two daughters.

"I wish they were here too. Then I wouldn't have to watch it with you all the time," Jaden said right as his phone started ringing.

He frowned when he saw Tori's number pop up on the screen, but he ignored her call and focused his attention on the TV. When she called right back Jaden was ready to go off, but he couldn't do that in front of his daughter.

"Get up for a second and let me run to the bathroom right quick baby," Jaden said to his daughter who was lounging comfortably on his chest. He hurriedly walked to his bedroom and closed the door before he picked up.

"You must want me to come to your sister's house and choke your stupid ass to death," Jaden threatened when he answered the phone.

"What did I do now?" Tori asked like she was clueless.

"I told you to stop calling my phone. You act like you got a fucking mental problem," Jaden yelled.

"I know what you said, but it's not like Kia is around," Tori replied.

"You don't know if she's here or not," Jaden argued.

"I know she's not there because I just saw her truck. And yes I'm sure that it was hers because her front plate is a picture of you and Jaylynn," Tori said as if she could read his mind.

Jaden calmed down a little, but he was still wondering what her stupid ass was calling him for. She had enough product to last for a while.

"What do you want Tori?" He inquired.

"I want to see you," she whined like a little ass girl.

"See me for what? It's not time for us to meet up to discuss nothing."

"I'm not talking about seeing you like that. I want to spend time with you," Tori clarified.

"That ain't happening. I already told you that I'm not on that with you no more," Jaden replied.

"But why? I told you that I was sorry about calling Kia's phone and stuff."

"It's not even about that Tori. I should have never mixed business with pleasure. I knew that shit was going to turn out bad. And how the fuck did you get all the way in Slidell anyway? You got a rental car?" Jaden questioned.

"What? I'm not in Slidell. I'm uptown with my people about to go to the tattoo shop," she replied.

"Well, where did you see Kia's car?" Jaden inquired.

"Uptown on St. Charles," she replied making him heated.

"Where at on St. Charles?"

"It was parked in Houston's parking lot," she said referring to a popular restaurant.

"Cool, but let me call you right back," Jaden said as he hung up the phone. He was pissed as he rummaged through his dresser in search of some comfortable clothing. Kia was on some bullshit just like he'd said from the beginning.

"Jay, you wanna go spend the night with your uncle Bryce and your cousins?" Jaden opened the door and yelled to his daughter.

"Yes!" Jaylynn shouted as she ran into the room with a big smile on her face.

"Okay, go pack you a bag and let's go."

"I already have clothes at Uncle Bryce's house," Jay replied.

"Alright, well go make sure that everything is straightened up before we go."

"Okay," Jaylynn yelled as she skipped out of the room.

Jaden grabbed his keys from the dresser and headed to the front of the house. Kia had him all the way fucked up with the games that she was trying to play. She wanted the old Jaden back and she was about to get that nigga.

Chapter 12

"Ooh, yes, right there," Kia moaned in satisfaction. "You're about to make me cum."

It felt like her body started to convulse as a wave of pleasure took over. She screamed out in pleasure as her companion continued to suck and lick every part of her womanhood like a starving man. Once she came again she tried to push his head away from her sensitive area, but he wasn't budging.

"Oh my God Andre. Stop, I can't take no more," Kia begged while almost kicking him away from her.

He lifted his head and smirked cockily just like he always did. Kia was always talking about how much she loved oral sex, but she couldn't take it once he gave it to her. He wanted to do more than just lick on her, but she wasn't ready for that just yet. She was so in love with the nigga that she had at home, but he was trying to change that. Obviously he wasn't doing right by her because this was her third weekend creeping off with him.

"You good?" Andre asked her.

Kia was one of prettiest girls that he'd ever been with and he wanted to make things official. She didn't lie about her relationship status and he respected that about her. They never got into details about her man, but Andre really didn't want to.

"Yeah," she panted as she tried to regulate her breathing. "What time is it?"

"It's almost eleven," Andre replied.

"Shit!" Kia yelled as she jumped up from the bed. "I have to get going. I didn't know that it was that late."

"Time flies when you're having fun," Andre winked at her.

"I know, but I have to go. I promised my sister that I would pick her up from work. She's been staying with me and Jaden."

"Okay. Am I going to see you again next weekend?" Andre asked as he started putting his clothes on. It was a waste for him to get naked because nothing ever happened besides him going down on her. He was hopeful that she would ask for more one day, but that time never came.

"I'll try, but I don't want Jaden to start getting suspicious. He asked me a million questions today before I left," Kia replied.

"Can't you just tell him that you have to work this weekend or something?" Andre asked.

"I haven't worked weekends in three years. Trust me, he's far from stupid. This is the calmest that my relationship with him has ever been and I want to keep it that way," Kia replied as she applied some gloss to her lips.

She checked her appearance in the mirror to make sure she was on point before following Andre out of the room.

"Just see what you can do. I want to see you again next weekend. That's my only days off too," Andre replied.

"Okay, I'll try, but I can't make any promises," Kia said as they walked to his truck hand in hand. She rode with Andre to the hotel room, but he was bringing her back to her car that she left at the restaurant.

"I'll take that," Andre smiled as he opened the door for her to get in. Once he was safely inside he pulled away from the hotel and headed in the opposite direction to bring Kia to her car.

***

"Man, I'm not trying to go to jail messing around with you bruh," Shawn said as he looked over at Jaden who was relaxing comfortably with a beer in his passenger's seat.

When his cousin called and asked him to drive him somewhere his first reaction was to say no. Jaden had always been there for him, so he didn't feel right turning him down. After dropping Jaylynn of at Bryce's house, they proceeded to a restaurant that Jaden believed Kia to be at. They spotted her car in the parking lot, but she was nowhere to be found when Jaden went inside to look for her. His crazy ass even went into the women's bathroom even though Shawn begged him not to. They'd been sitting outside in his car for almost two hours, but Kia still hadn't shown up.

"Chill out with your scary ass. They got cameras out here nigga. I'm not new to this shit," Jaden replied making him breathe a little easier.

"You need to just confront her when she gets home. It don't make no sense to wait out here and you don't know where she's at or what time she's coming back."

"Confront her with what. I ain't see shit yet. Her car being parked here don't mean nothing to me. She can easily lie and said she rode with one of her girls. I need some solid proof before I react. And best believe I'm gonna react," Jaden said matter-of-factly.

Shawn fidgeted nervously in his seat because he didn't know what was to come. Jaden was just like his father and they thought of shit that normal people would have never imagined. Shawn remembered Shaq getting into it with one of their neighbors when he was younger over a parking spot. He didn't know how his father found out that the other man was allergic to bees, but he used that bit of information to his advantage. One day when the man got into his car, Shaq threw a jar full of bees through his window while he and Jaden blocked him from getting out of the car. It took ten minutes for someone to help the poor man out, but he was unconscious by the time they did. He stayed in the hospital for over a week, but thankfully he didn't die. He packed his family up moved away from the area after that. Everybody in the neighborhood knew what happened, but they were too afraid of Shaq to say anything. He was feared by many and so was Jaden.

"It's show time nigga," Jaden said pulling Shawn from his thoughts of the past. Shawn looked up right as an all-black Ford F-150 pulled up next to Kia's car and parked.

"Bruh just chill. Don't get out of the car. Watch and see what happens first," Shawn suggested.

Jaden had no intentions of getting out, so he ignored everything that his cousin was saying. He smirked when he saw a tall dark skinned man with dreads get out of the car and open the door for Kia. He and Shawn were parked all the way to the back of the parking lot so they had a perfect view of everything. When the man hugged Kia and kissed her on the cheek, his smirk faded just like his common sense at the moment.

"Ole hot pussy ass," Jaden fumed as he watched Kia backing out of her parking space. Her male companion waited until she left before he got back into his truck and backed out soon after. Jaden now knew that he was one of her co-workers.

The University of New Orleans staff parking sticker on the back of his truck was a dead giveaway because Kia had the exact same one.

"Follow that nigga," Jaden demanded calmly.

"Man..." Shawn was about to object until Jaden went off on him.

"Nigga just do what the fuck I said. I don't know why I even deal with your scary ass. Your daddy's name alone put fear in nigga's hearts and you walking around here acting like a lil bitch," Jaden snapped.

"You can say what you want about me. I ain't never been to jail before and I'm not trying to go now. You on your own if some shit pop off. I'm making that clear to you right now," Shawn said while pulling off and tailing the unknown man.

"Nigga I wouldn't do no dirt with you if you paid me. I'll take Quell with me first," Jaden said referring to Shawn's sister.

"Quell?" Shawn questioned like he was offended.

"Yeah nigga, your sister. She got more heart than you. That's Shaq's daughter for sure. He need to get a blood test done on your punk ass," Jaden replied.

They continued the rest of the drive in silence until the man that they were following pulled up to some apartments on Tulane Avenue. It wasn't far from the hospital where he worked so that was a plus for Jaden. There was a security gate surrounding the complex so he instructed Shawn to drive in right after him. They followed him to a building and watched as he parked in an assigned parking spot. Jaden waited until he got out and went inside before he got out of the car. He looked at the number on the door of the apartment and compared it to the number that the truck was parked in to make sure they matched. Once he was satisfied, he walked back to Shawn's car and instructed him to drive him home. Kia's timing was almost perfect because she called Jaden's phone as soon as he and Shawn drove away.

"What's up baby?" Jaden said when he answered the phone.

"Nothing, I'm on my way to pick Keller up," she replied.

Jaden had forgotten all about Keller staying with them. He was so busy trying to get at Kia that he didn't think about anybody else. As long as his daughter was gone he thought it was all good. He thought he was going to have to wait to confront her, but what Kia said next had him ready to go through with his plans once again.

"I have to drop her off at her friend's house and then I'll be home," Kia added.

"Okay baby, I'll see you then," Jaden said before they disconnected. That was just enough time for him to get home and wait for her. They had to talk, but he wasn't trying to do any time soon. He had something else planned for her hot ass. Something that was sure to calm her down for a while.

Chapter 13

A hot shower and a bed was all that Kia craved. After dropping Keller off at Tessa's house, she filled her gas tank up and headed home. Andre called to make sure that she was straight and she assured him that she was. He knew not to call or text once she got inside because Jaden was nobody to play with. Andre claimed he wasn't scared of anybody, but she could guarantee that he'd never met anybody like Jaden Andrews. Some battles just weren't worth fighting and that was one of them. She felt bad about creeping on Jaden, but she was sick of his shit. He did whatever he wanted to do whenever he felt like doing it and she was tired of sitting back taking it. For some strange reason she felt like she was getting back at him for the all the times that he cheated on her. It was childish as hell, but it felt damn good. Even still, Kia could never see herself leaving her first love. As crazy as he was, Jaden was good to her and their daughter. If only he could keep his dick in his pants he would be the perfect mate.

"God Jaden, it's freezing in here," Kia said when she entered the house.

She found Jaden relaxing on the sofa with a beer like he

didn't feel a thing. She walked down the hall to check on her daughter and make sure that she was properly covered up. When she saw that Jaylynn wasn't in her bed she assumed that she'd fallen asleep in theirs.

"Is Jay in our bed?" Kia asked.

"Nah, she's staying the night with Bryce and Taylor," Jaden replied as he walked over to her. Kia tensed up when he pulled her into a hug because she didn't know how far he wanted to go. She couldn't have sex with Jaden while she still had another man's scent on her. She and Andre didn't have sex, but there was still some form of intimacy that took place.

"I need to take a shower. You wanna watch a movie when I'm done?" Kia asked trying to distract him from wanting sex.

"Yeah, that's cool," Jaden replied while giving her a peck on her lips. Kia was nervous even though she tried her best to hide it. He knew her like a book, so there was no need for her to pretend. He sensed it the minute she entered the house.

"You gotta turn that air down baby. I'll catch a cold if I get out of the shower and it's freezing like this," Kia said as she walked away to their bedroom.

Jaden watched as she stripped down out of everything that she had on and went to the bathroom. He got heated just imagining another man being somewhere that only he'd had the privilege of being. It infuriated him to know that another man had even seen her naked. The first one didn't live to tell about it, but this new nigga was a new problem for him. No matter how much dirt Jaden did, he was selfish when it came to Kia. As soon as she walked into the bathroom, Jaden grabbed her phone and unlocked it. Kia was known for taking long showers because she listened to her music while she did. Jaden had purchased her a shower head with a built in Bluetooth. She kept her iPod in the bathroom cabinet, so she always turned it on before she took her showers.

"Slick ass bitch," Jaden said as he scrolled through Kia's phone.

She had her co-worker Andrea's name in the phone twice with two different phone numbers. It didn't take long for Jaden to figure out who the real Andrea was and who was the decoy. Kia and her co-worker Andrea only talked about work. The other number that was saved under her name was a different story. According to those messages, Kia and ole boy had hooked up at least two other times besides that night. That was who she had been with when she claimed to have been with her friends from work the two weekends prior. Jaden went through every message between the two of them and got madder with each one that he read. It wasn't until he got to the most current ones that he really got heated. The nigga was telling Kia that he loved how she tasted, but he was ready to take it to the next level. Jaden was happy that she didn't have sex with him, but he was still pissed that she even let him go down on her. Oral sex was Kia's weakness and Jaden knew that. That's why he made it his business to please her orally even on the days that they didn't have sex. He didn't want her to go out and get it from another man, but she ended up doing that anyway on more than one occasion. He even got her right before she left, but that obviously wasn't enough for her hot ass.

"Corny ass nigga," Jaden mumbled as he continued to read the messages.

He chuckled when he read the part about him telling Kia that she tasted like a bag of skittles. That was some shit that grown men just didn't say. After having read enough, Jaden was ready to get down to business. He went to their storage closet out back and grabbed the commercial blower. He had their central air turned on fifty, but he turned it to forty when he got back inside. After plugging the blower up to a long extension cord, Jaden grabbed the broom and unscrewed the stick from the brush. Armed with the stick in one hand and the blower in the other, Jaden opened the bathroom door and walked in. Kia had the music up loud as she sang along with Chris Brown's Royalty Album. Jaden took the broom stick and jammed one side of the shower door so that only one side could fully open. Kia's eyes were closed when he opened the other side of the glass door and that was perfect for him. After turning the blower on high, Jaden turned off the hot water and pointed the blower directly towards Kia's naked boy.

"Ooooh shit! Jaden, the hot water went out!" Kia screamed. She had moisturizer covering her face and eyes, so she didn't even realize what was going on.

"I turned it off. Your hot pussy ass need to cool down," Jaden replied.

"Wh...What are you talking about?" Kia asked as she shivered and reached for her towel to wipe her face. Once she saw what was going on, she backed away and tried to get out from the opposite end of the shower.

"Don't even try it. This is your only way out and that ain't happening either," Jaden taunted.

"Oh my God Jaden. Turn that blower off. Are you fucking crazy?"

"Yeah, but you already knew that. So tell me Kia, where were you tonight?" he asked her.

"I already told you where I was," she replied as her teeth chattered.

"Wrong answer!" Jaden yelled as he pointed the water nozzle at her, spraying her with the freezing cold water.

"Ahh! Okay, I was with my co-worker," Kia said barely above a whisper.

"Keep going, I'm listening," Jaden demanded.

"Nothing happened Jaden, I swear," Kia yelled.

"Keep lying to me if you want to. I'll have your hot ass laid up in the hospital with pneumonia. I'll come visit your ass every day like I don't know what the fuck happened to you," Jaden threatened.

"I didn't have sex with him," Kia blurted out.

"I already know that, I checked your phone. I wanna know who this nigga is and how long you been dealing with his ass."

"His name is Andre and he's a surgical tech at the hospital. We always eat lunch together and he asked me out to dinner," Kia answered in a hurry.

"Andre huh?" Jaden smirked at how close his name really was to Andrea's

"Yes, that's his name, I swear," Kia yelled.

"So you going on dates and shit like you ain't got a man at home. What kind of bullshit is that? Nigga talking about you taste like candy and shit."

"I'm sorry Jaden. Just please turn off the water and that blower," Kia begged as she shivered like crazy.

Since Jaden had all of the information that he needed he turned the water and blower off. He threw Kia a big towel and watched as she hurriedly covered up her wet, cold body. Her bottom lip was trembling and tears were pouring from her eyes.

"And don't even think about looking for that phone. How the fuck you gon' talk to another nigga on some shit that I pay the bill on? You got me fucked up," Jaden fumed as he walked away and slammed the door behind him.

Usually Kia would be yelling for him to get out, but she was in the wrong that time. She knew that what she and Andre had wouldn't last forever, but she didn't think it would end the way it did. She really wanted to apologize to Jaden again, but he was too pissed off for her to approach him. Once she dried herself off, Kia slipped on a pair of long sleeved pajama's and cuddled under the covers. She knew that Andre would probably text her before the weekend was over. Unfortunately it would be Jaden that got the messages instead of her.

Chapter 14

Being away from Leo for three weeks proved to be exactly what Keller needed. She really missed him, but she needed him to miss her too. He needed to see exactly how it felt to be without her. Between spending nights at Kia and Tessa's houses, Keller was ready to be back in her on bed. Then again, she was enjoying her freedom and the time that she got to spend with Tigga. Keller didn't tell him or anyone else the entire story of what happened. The only thing everybody knew was that she and Leo got into it and she left for a little while. Leo was going crazy as usual. He called Keller every five minutes or he popped up at the shop whenever he felt like it. Keller had so many gifts delivered to the shop that she forgot to take some of them home most of the time.

"You want me to make you some more soup sis?" Keller asked Kia.

After staying at Tessa'a house for two nights, she'd come back to Kia's house the night before to find her sick as a dog with a terrible cold. Jaden had it looking like a hospital room with all the medicine and the two humidifiers that he had plugged up. Keller didn't know what had happened on the two nights that she was gone, but she could tell that Jaden and Kia weren't on speaking terms. They walked by each other like two strangers.

"I'm good. It ain't like I can taste that shit anyway," Kia replied breathing through her nose.

"I know they were shocked as hell when you called off from work," Keller said.

"Hell yeah, but they told me to take as much time as I needed. I got a million sick hours. Aside from vacations, I've never used any of my time since I've been there," she replied.

"Well, I'm about to get going. Tessa is coming to get me since she's my first client of the day," Keller informed her.

"You need to think about getting your own car Keller. What couple do you know still shares a car these days? Leo made sure he put that shit in his name so he can keep it whenever y'all break up."

"Everything is in his name because he pays for it," Keller said.

"That's my point. You're making decent money and you get to keep all of it since he pays the bills. You need to get you a car. You have good credit so that shouldn't be a problem," Kia replied.

"You make a good point sis," Keller admitted.

"I hope you're saving some of that money and not blowing it all."

"I know better than that Kia. You know Mo drilled that in us at an early age," Keller replied.

"She sure did. That's why my savings is sitting pretty," Kia admitted.

"Mine is too, but you're right. I need to get me another car. I've been without one for two years."

Keller had an Audi until it was stolen and wrecked. Her insurance company totaled it out and cut her a check. Instead of getting another car she deposited the money into her savings and shared a car with Leo.

"You can let one of our uncles go with you. They know how to wheel and deal," Kia said right as she coughed and sneezed back to back.

"God bless you," Keller said while handing her sister a tissue.

"Thanks," Kia smile weakly.

"You look and sound just awful," Keller informed her.

"Thanks again," Kia replied sarcastically.

"You know you're still cute boo. Just not right now," Keller said as she jumped back to keep from being hit with the dirty tissues that her sister threw at her.

"Bye heifer. I'll see you later," Kia said right before her sister walked out of the bedroom.

Keller laughed when she walked into the living room and saw Jaden and Jaylynn lounging on the sofa watching Matilda. Poor Jaden must have watched that movie every day more than one time a day. He was such a great father and he never complained. Just like Kia, he'd taken a few days off from work to stay home and take care of her. Keller felt like he was such a good man to her sister, but Kia felt otherwise. According to her it was Jaden's fault that she was sick to begin with.

"Where's the keys to the deadbolt?" Keller asked aloud.

The keys usually stayed in the door, but she couldn't find them anywhere when she really needed them. Tessa was outside waiting on her and she needed to get going.

"You can't leave out of the house Tee Keller," Jaylynn said while never taking her eyes off of the TV.

"What? Why can't I leave?" Keller questioned.

"Because we're on lockdown. That means that nobody can leave out of the house," Jaylynn replied like it was a normal occurrence.

"What kind of mess is that?" Keller yelled as she walked back to her sister's bedroom and burst through the door.

"What's wrong?" Kia asked her.

"Bitch I don't know, but I don't have time for this shit. What does Jaylynn mean about the house being on lockdown?" Keller quizzed.

"Shit," Kia hissed as she pulled the covers off and stood up. "I told you that you should have stayed by Tessa for a little while. Jaden is back on his psycho bullshit."

"I have to go to work Kia. I can't play these crazy ass games with Jaden today."

"I know Keller. I'll get him to let you out. This bitch act like he's shell shocked and ain't never been to war before," Kia fussed.

Keller followed her sister to the living room and stood right next to her.

"You feel better mama?" Jaylynn looked up and asked her.

"Yeah baby, I'm feeling much better," Kia lied. She actually felt like shit, but she couldn't tell that to her baby.

"Jaden, Keller has to go to work," Kia said to her crazy ass boyfriend.

Jaden continued watching the movie without even looking over at them.

"We're on lockdown mama. Nobody can leave out of the house. Right daddy," Jaylynn said while looking up at her father.

"That's right baby," Jaden smiled down at her.

"Baby please, her ride is outside waiting on her," Kia continued to beg.

When Jaden continued to ignore them Keller was about to lose it. She knew that popping off at the mouth would only make things worse, so she tried to be as nice as she could.

"Jaden please, just let me out and you can lock up again. Why the hell am I on lockdown anyway? I don't even know what's going on." Keller pouted.

"Your sister can get you out of here. As soon as she does what she has to do," Jaden said calmly.

"God Jaden, I said I was sorry a thousand times. Just let Keller out and we can talk about this later," Kia begged.

Once again, Jaden turned his head and completely ignored them. Keller didn't know what was infuriating her the most. Jaden's calmness or the fact that she was damn near thirty and being punished by her younger sister's boyfriend.

"Kia, help me get out of here. What do you have to do?" Keller yelled.

"Ugh!!" Kia groaned as she stormed off to the bedroom with Keller following close behind her.

"My ride is going to leave me. I can't believe this shit," Keller said as she flopped down on the bed in defeat.

"Let me see your phone," Kia requested.

Keller slid her phone over to her sister as she continued to sulk. She heard Kia on the phone with their phone service provider, but she didn't know what she was doing. She had tuned her out until she said something that got her attention.

"Come on so you can get to work," Kia said while heading back to the living room.

"How when G.I Joe got it locked down like Fort Knox?" Keller replied.

"He's about to let you out. Just come on," Kia replied.

Keller didn't believe her, but she followed her out anyway.

"Here," Kia said handing Jaden a piece of paper. "This is my new number."

He took the paper from her and dialed the number on his cell phone. When Kia's phone started ringing in his pocket, he nodded in satisfaction. Kia refused to get her number changed when he told her to, but Jaden had a way of getting what he wanted. She hated that her sister got caught in the middle, but Keller was probably use to his craziness by now. Andre had been calling and texting Kia's phone non-stop, but Jaden and been holding it down. He entertained the other man for a little while to get some information from him, but he had grown tired of playing the game. He now knew Andre's schedule and everything else that he wanted to know. Kia had no use for her old number and he let her know it. Keller stood there with her mouth open wide as Jaden reached into his back pocket and handed Kia the keys to the deadbolt.

"Is the lockdown over daddy?" Jaylynn asked her father.

"Yeah baby, everything is back to normal," Jaden replied.

"I'm sorry about that sis," Kia said to Keller. Once she opened the door, Keller all but ran to Tessa's car and jumped inside.

"Girl I thought you changed your mind on me. What the hell is wrong with you?" Tessa questioned.

"Bitch I don't care if I have to sleep with one eye open. I'm bringing my ass back home tonight," Keller swore.

Tessa didn't ask any more questions because it seemed like Keller had a lot on her mind. Tessa turned up her radio and drove over to the shop. It was early and Tessa was happy that she was Keller's first customer. Keller's clientele was picking up and her slow days had started to be busy as well. They walked into the shop and spoke to everyone before walking to Keller's work area. A huge smile covered her face when she saw the huge stuffed bear and the dozen pink roses that awaited her. Leo was really trying hard to win her back and Tessa wondered what he'd done to lose her in the first place.

"I'm going to the bathroom right quick," Tessa said to her smiling friend.

"Okay," Keller continued to smile.

"Baby you've been getting deliveries just about every day this week. What was it this time, cheating or beating?" Co-Co asked making Keller's smile fade instantly.

"Why do you always do that Co-Co? You act like you hate to see a bitch happy," Keller spat angrily.

"Happy or not I just hate to see a dumb bitch," Co-Co said matter-of factly.

Keller ignored his negative remarks and read the card that accompanied her flowers. She was almost in tears as she read what Leo had written. He poured his heart out to her and begged for another chance. He promised to get it right and even said that he was willing to go to counseling for his anger. His begging wasn't in vain though. Right before she started to work on Tessa, Keller sent him a text informing him that she would be home right after work. She just hoped she was making the right decision and was walking into the lion's den yet again

Chapter 15

Three days later Jaden and his cousin Quell were sitting outside of Andre's apartment waiting for him to come home. Jaden knew that he was most likely at the gym according to the schedule that he provided via text message to who he thought was Kia.

"Skittles huh cuz?" Quell laughed as she repeated what Jaden had told her earlier about Andre. She couldn't believe that his dumb ass had compared Kia's woman parts to candy.

"Yep, and I'm a make sure his bitch taste the rainbow. That's one pussy he gon' be sorry that he put his mouth on. That niggas taste buds will never be the same again," Jaden swore.

"Is Kia feeling any better?" Quell asked.

"She's still not feeling good, but my mama and Brooklyn are at the house with her," he replied.

"Cool, but what's up with this nigga that we're waiting on? You trying to finish him or what" Quell inquired.

"Not at all. Shit not even that serious with me. Honestly, I was gon' let the nigga make it until he sent that bullshit ass text before Kia got her number changed."

"What text?" Quell questioned.

"This nigga was bold as fuck talking bout coming to my

house to check on her and shit. Somebody at the job told him that she was sick and he wanted to bring her some soup and stuff. Nigga was talking about asking a female co-worker to come with him to throw me off and everything," Jaden chuckled.

"Are you serious?" Quell asked while laughing with him.

"Dead ass. I started to tell his ass to come through. I would have beat the fuck out of him when he did. If it wasn't for my baby being there that's exactly what would have went down."

"That nigga is crazy."

"Yeah and so am I," Jaden countered.

Quell would never dispute that because it was true. Jaden was like a younger version of her father. Shaq must have seen something in his nephew because he instantly favored him over all of the others. Let Shawn tell it, Shaq even favored Jaden over him. Quell was often Jaden's accomplice when he did his dirt, so she knew that he was really about that life. Whoever that Andre character was should have been happy that he was still breathing right now. Jaden loved Kia like an inmate loved their freedom, and he didn't play when it came to her.

"My toy just pulled up and I'm ready to play," Jaden said when he saw a black F-150 pull into a parking spot across from where they were parked.

Quell watched as Jaden pulled his gun from her glove box and put in the pocket of his black hoodie. He got out of the car and slowly walked over to the man who he had been waiting to see. Quell got out behind him, but she stayed a few feet away from him to watch his back. They'd already checked the area for cameras and were pleased to see that there were none around.

"What's up bruh? Andre right?" Jaden said by way of greeting.

"Uh, yeah and you are?" Andre questioned.

"You don't know me, but we have something in common," Jaden replied.

"And what's that?" Andre asked.

"We both like the way my girl's pussy taste," Jaden frowned as he pulled out his gun and slammed it across Andre's face.

"Ughh," Andre groaned in pain as he went down to the ground. The blow caught him off guard, but he still tried to fight back. He didn't have to wonder who Jaden was. His last comment let him know exactly who he was and why he was there.

"Oh this lil bitch trying to fight back," Jaden said seemingly amused when Andre caught him in the jaw with a weak left hook.

"Punish that nigga cuz," Quell instigated from the sidelines.

She didn't have to encourage Jaden because punishing Andre was exactly what he intended to do. Jaden was determined to knock out every teeth that Andre had in his mouth. He used the butt of his gun to repeatedly hit his much bigger opponent in the mouth. Quell cringed when she saw all of the blood and condition of Andre's face. Jaden said he didn't want to kill him, but that's exactly what was going to happen if she didn't stop. Andre was a tough one though. He was still conscious after all that he was enduring at the hands of his attacker.

"Alright fam, let him make it. He got your point," Quell said while pulling Jaden away.

"You ain't bout that life nigga!" Jaden barked angrily as he put his bloody weapon back in his pocket.

"I'm calling the police," Andre mumbled almost inaudibly through his swollen lips and battered face.

Quell didn't know if some of Andre's teeth were in the puddle of blood that he'd spit out or not, but she was sure that he was missing some after that beating. His movements were slow as he reached into the pockets of his sweat pants, but Jaden didn't seem to be fazed.

"You can get the police involved if you want to, but you'll regret it before I do. Nobody in your family will be safe when I get through with your punk as. Your mama in Lakeview and your sisters and brother on Airline Highway can get it too," Jaden threatened.

All of Andre's movements ceased after Jaden mentioned his family and where they lived. Kia always said that he was crazy, but that was putting it mildly. Andre liked her, but not enough to risk his life and the lives of his family. Whatever they had ended the moment Jaden's gun collided with his face.

"I'm done," Andre whispered.

"Say what nigga?" Jaden asked as he cupped his hand over his ear and leaned in closer.

"I said I'm done fucking with Kia. Just please leave my family out of this," Andre begged.

"Nah nigga, you leave your family out of this. Don't fuck with mine and I won't fuck with yours," Jaden countered.

"I'm done, I swear. You have my word," Andre promised.

"You keep your word and you get to keep your life. Go back on your word and you're a dead man," Jaden cautioned right before he casually walked away and got back into Quell's car.

She wasted no time pulling away from the apartment complex and driving towards the bridge to bring Jaden home. He seemed to have gotten his point across and he probably wouldn't be hearing from Andre ever again.

"How did you find out all of that information about his family?" Quell asked as she and Jaden drove across the bridge.

"How do you think I found out?" Jaden quizzed.

"Kia?" Quell verified just to be sure.

"Yep," he confirmed. "See, the thing these niggas need to understand is that Kia is loyal. She might slip up and get her a lil head action every now and then, but when shit hits the fan she's Team Jaden without a doubt."

"I see that. I thought she was gon' put you out again after you tried to turn her into a Popsicle," Quell laughed.

"Y'all really think Kia be putting me out huh?" Jaden asked. "Whenever I leave that house it's because I want to. That's Jaylynn's comfort zone. I know if I don't leave for a little while then Kia probably will. I'm not trying to make my baby uncomfortable like that."

"That's what up cuz," Quell nodded.

"Now I gotta go home and start the ass kissing process," Jaden admitted.

"What are you planning to do to make up with her this time?"

"I don't know. Maybe we'll take a family vacation or something. Kia's been asking to go back to New York. Maybe I'll take her and Jaylynn there for a few days."

"You can be prepared to go broke for that trip."

"I already know. But if it makes my two favorite girls happy then it's all good with me," he replied as he dialed Kia number to tell her that he was on his way.

Chapter 16

"Hey boo, you look cute today," Co-Co complimented Keller when she walked into the salon.

"Thanks honey," Keller smiled at him.

"The fuck you be walking around here with that goofy ass smile on your face all day for?" Jaden asked her.

"Shut up Jaden. Is it a crime for me to be happy?" Keller asked him.

"I wonder why," Jaden said giving her the side eye.

He knew that Keller and Tigga hooked up with each other from time to time, but she was still with Leo's no good grimy ass. Jaden didn't care for him that much, but he was cordial with him because of his sister-in-law. Keller was like another sister to him because they had been around each other almost their entire lives. He liked Tigga for her, but it wasn't his decision to make. Tigga was cool and Jaden hung out with him and his brother-in-law Dominic a few times. The nigga was running a multi-million dollar construction company and he wasn't even thirty years old yet.

"It's not even like that, so get your mind out of the gutter. Me and my man are good. I haven't talked to Tigga in a few weeks," Keller replied.

Aside from seeing Tigga when he came to the shop to get his hair cut, Keller hadn't really had any communication with him. She'd been back home with Leo for a little over a month and they were doing fine. True to his word, Leo had never raised his hand to her since she'd been back home. Keller was genuinely happy for the first time in a while.

"Why haven't you been talking to Tigga?" Candace questioned.

"Because," Keller drawled. "Me and Leo are doing good and I don't want anything to jeopardize that."

"Bitch please, that's like turning down steak and potatoes for ham and cheese. By right, Leo needs to be single. His ass is too ugly to be in a relationship," Co-Co chimed in.

"What does his looks have to do with anything? I know that he doesn't look the best, but I don't see his outer appearance when I look at him," Keller defended.

"That bitch is blind," Co-Co said making Candace and his client laugh.

"I'm a man so another nigga's looks don't mean shit to me. It's all about how he treats you. You can't pay me to believe that Leo treats you better than Tigga," Jaden spoke up.

"Says the man who puts his entire house on lockdown," Keller replied sarcastically.

"I just got a different way of doing shit, but Kia and Jaylynn are straight," Jaden answered.

"Kia is very straight after that New York shopping spree," Candace replied.

Although Kia was wrong, Jaden wanted to bury the hatchet and do something nice for her and their daughter. Since Kia had been asking to go back to New York, he flew her and Jaylynn there for an entire week. He knew that Kia was going to hit his pockets to get back at him and he was right. He spent close to twenty thousand dollars on her and Jaylynn, but it was cool. They did so much shopping that he had to rent a van for them to drive back home. It was a long ass drive, but there was way that they could have flown with all of the items that they had purchased. As soon as Jaden got back home, he called Tori and Serena to start putting in extra work for him.

"I saw all that stuff that her and Jaylynn came back with," Keller said pulling Jaden out of his daydream.

"You need to get on the winning team. Tigga got them coins," Co-Co said.

"How do you know that Co-Co? You only know him from coming in here," Keller replied.

"That nigga look like money. I've been around long enough to know," Co-Co said confidently.

"You better listen to Co-Co. He's one of the original hoes from way back in the day," Jaden blurted out with a straight face.

"No your cry baby ass didn't bitch. Don't make me tell everybody how you came crying to me that last time Kia broke up with you," Co-Co shrieked.

"Oh, so you wanna hit below the belt?" Jaden yelled back. "How about you tell them how your feminine ass came crying to me when you thought Dwight gave you a disease. Nigga had a hair bump on his lil dick and swore that he was dying. He wanted me to kill Dwight and the man ain't even do shit."

They had the entire shop weak with laughter after that. That was the reason why Keller loved her job the most. There was never a dull moment with the characters that she worked with.

"Now that's messed up Jaden. I told you that in confidence," Co-Co whined.

"I came to you in confidence too. I'm not ashamed to say that I shed a few tears over Kia. Real niggas cry too," Jaden replied right as Tessa walked through the door.

She stopped and spoke to everybody before walking to Keller's work area.

"Girl you just missed the funniest shit that you've probably ever heard before in your life," Keller told Tessa once they sat down at her work station.

"Must have been Co-Co and Jaden," Tessa assumed.

"You already know," Keller said as she told her what happened.

It didn't take long before Tessa was doubled over in laughter as well. She loved coming to the shop and she made sure that her schedule was free and clear so that she could stay for a while when she did. She didn't even have to get anything done at the moment, but she wanted to chill with her friend and get a few laughs in for a little while.

"I wish you could come with us weekend after next. You still have plenty of time to clear your schedule," Tessa said to Keller once again.

They were going to Tigga's vacation property in Florida and she had been begging Keller to come along with them. Aside from Tigga and their mother, Anaya and the kids were tagging along too. Tigga was pissed that Anaya was going, but the kids seemed to be excited about it.

"Clearing my schedule is never a problem. If me and Leo were still broken up I would have been on the first thing smoking out of here. He would go crazy if I went out of town without him," Keller said right as the door chimed alerting them of a visitor.

When she saw Tori walk in she knew that it was about to be some unnecessary drama. She could tell that Jaden was heated as he turned his angry glare towards his unwanted visitor.

"What the fuck you want Tori?" Jaden snapped irritably.

"I want the rest of my money that you never paid me. I'm not Serena. You can't pay me when you feel like it and expect me to be okay with it," Tori replied with her hand on her hips.

"Girl you better get the fuck on," Jaden chuckled even though he didn't find anything funny. He and Kia had just gotten their relationship back on track and he didn't need Tori and her drama interfering with that.

"I'm not going nowhere until you pay me my money," Tori said defiantly.

"Tori I'm telling you to chill. Don't come to my job with that bullshit," Jaden warned again. Keller knew the look in his eyes all too well. That was the calm before the storm and Tori needed to keep it pushing.

"Fuck that! You got money to take your bitch on shopping sprees in New York. You need to pay me my money or find somebody else to sell your shit."

Tori knew that she was playing with fire when she showed up to Jaden's job, but she didn't care. It pissed her off when she looked on Kia's social media accounts and saw that Jaden had taken her and their daughter to New York. She posted hundreds of pictures of them shopping and having fun like one big happy family. That bitch Kia was cocky with it too. Her pages weren't even private because she wanted everybody to see. Tori could care less about the two hundred dollars that he owed her. Jaden blew more than that on games for Jaylynn, so she knew that he had it. The money was just her reason for showing up there in the first place. It was a decision that she was sure to regret. She had barely gotten the last word out of her mouth before Jaden's hands were wrapped around her throat.

"Jaden no!" Co-Co yelled as he and Candace tried to pull their cousin off of his crazy stalker. Jaden was too strong for them because he didn't let up. Keller and Tessa watched in horror as Jaden lifted Tori off of her feet and tossed her out of the shop and onto the concrete.

"Stupid bitch," Jaden yelled as he reached into his pocket and pulled out two crisps hundred dollar bills and threw them at her. "You better make that shit last cause I'm done with you. I'll find somebody else to work with."

Tori knew how to handle Jaden's business, but he didn't need the extra drama that came along with her. His uncle Shaq was working on trying to get him somebody else, but he hadn't had any luck so far. Sheena was still doing her thing for him, but she couldn't do it all alone. Jaden hated to get his hands dirty again, but he would do whatever he needed to do in order to get rid of Tori.

"Jaden wait, I'm sorry," Tori screamed as she tried to get up and go after him.

"Baby girl you need to leave. That nigga almost broke every bone in your body and you're trying to chase after him," Co-Co said as he blocked her path.

"Jaden!" Tori screamed like the crazy bitch that she was.

Jaden ignored her, but Co-Co and Candace actually felt sorry for her. She obviously had some underlying issues that had nothing to do with their cousin. Tori wasn't wrapped too tight and that wasn't hard to see.

"Just let him calm down. He'll probably call you later," Candace said even though she knew that was a lie. She knew that a person had to handle girls like Tori a certain way or they would end up on an episode of Snapped.

"Okay, tell him that I said I'm sorry," Tori said as she wiped a few tears from her eyes.

"I will," Candace said as she watched her get into her rental car and pull off.

"Jaden better watch that bitch. She might pick Jaylynn up from school and take her to the amusement park like ole girl did on Fatal Attraction," Co-Co said making his sister laugh.

"Yeah, something ain't right with that one," Candace agreed as they walked back into the salon.

"You alright cousin?" Co-Co asked Jaden when they saw him sitting at Keller's work station. He was probably begging her not to tell Kia what had gone down just a few minutes ago.

"Yeah," Jaden replied with a scowl still plastered on his face.

Co-Co knew his cousin well enough to leave him alone when he was in one of those moods. Tori got off easy and she needed to know that. She could keep fucking with Jaden if she wanted to. Her family was going to be putting her crazy ass on the back of a few milk cartons and that much Co-Co was certain of.

Chapter 17

"How long are we gonna be staying in Florida?" Anaya asked Tigga when he walked into the kitchen. They barely said two words to each other most days and she had to find out from her six year old daughter that they were even going. When she did mention it to Tigga he seemed pissed that she had found out.

"I don't know. Why? It ain't like you got a job to get back to," he replied with a frown.

"I know I don't have a job, but it's not like I'm not looking. Why do you always have an attitude? I only asked so I'll know how much stuff to pack for me and the girls," Anaya replied.

"I really don't understand why you want to come. You don't even get along with my mama and sister like that."

"I don't have to say anything to your mama or Tessa. I'm going because my daughters are going."

"You ain't tired of pulling that same old card yet. That shit is really getting old," Tigga said in disgust.

"What's getting old?" Anaya asked.

"You using the kids to stay relevant is getting old. They're not cards and this is not a game. You can't keep using them thinking that you're gonna win," Tigga answered.

"I'm not using the kids to do anything," Anaya denied.

"I don't know why we're even still doing this same old song and dance. This relationship has been over for a long time. What are you trying to hold on to?" Tigga came right out and asked.

"What did I do that was so wrong to make you not want me anymore?" Anaya asked with tears in her eyes.

"Don't even try that crying shit. That's worn out too. We grew apart a long time ago and you know it. You getting pregnant with Amari is the only thing that held us together this long. I told you then that I wanted out, but your ass got comfortable. There's no love left between us. We don't even sleep in the same room anymore. It's like we're roommates."

"I do love you, so speak for yourself. It's like you woke up one morning and decided that you didn't want us anymore. Our kids don't deserve that," Anaya said as she wiped tears from her eyes.

"There is no us. I'll always want my kids. It's you that I'm done with," Tigga corrected.

"There is no them without me. You got me fucked up if you think another bitch is gonna help you raise my daughters. I'll take them away and make sure you don't see them again until they're grown," Anaya threatened just like always.

"That shit ain't working no more either. We're going before a judge this time. I'm not being forced to be with somebody that I don't wanna be with just to have a relationship with my kids. I should have never let this shit go on for this long."

"Why are you doing this to me?" Anaya whimpered.

"What am I doing to you? I've been trying to have this conversation with you for weeks, but you kept brushing me off. You thought that running from me was going to prolong the process, but you actually made it go faster."

"What process?" She asked angrily.

"I hope you enjoy your trip to Florida because this will be your last one. I'm moving into my new place when we come back. The rent is paid up on this apartment for the next six months, but you're on your own after that," Tigga said making her heart take a nosedive in her chest. Anaya wasn't expecting him to say that and she was definitely blindsided by the news. Somebody had to be in his ear and she knew that it was probably his mother or his sister.

"How can you do this to your daughters? Six months is not enough time for me to get on my feet and take care of them."

"I got them. You just worry about taking care of yourself."

"I won't even have to work when I'm done with you. I'm putting your ass on child support and nothing you can say will change my mind," Anaya promised.

"I figured you would and that's fine with me. I'll pay whatever the judge tells me to pay," Tigga said calmly.

No matter what Anaya said, his mind was made up. He had a damn good family lawyer thanks to his grandpa and he told Tigga exactly what to do. His grandpa had rental property in Metairie and he agreed to let him stay in one of his townhouses rent free until he was ready to buy him a home. Tigga had been thinking about making a move for months, and he felt better about it already. He just wanted his daughters to know that a separation from their mother was not a separation from them. He knew that Anaya was going to bad mouth him to his kids, but he was praying that they were smart enough to know the truth. He had a bond with his girls that he didn't want Anaya to break.

"Y'all come on. We're going by grandma for a little while," Anaya said to her daughters who were in the living room watching TV with their father.

"I don't wanna go," her oldest daughter started to moan and whine. It didn't take long before the other two followed her lead. Anaya was already frustrated and they weren't making it any better.

"Let's go! It ain't like he want y'all here anyway," Anaya yelled angrily.

Tigga jumped up from the sofa and pulled her outside and closed the front door behind them.

"You better not ever in your fucking life tell them no bullshit like that. You can feel however you want to feel, but don't bring my kids into this shit. You keep fucking with me and I'll have your ass back in that trailer park with your mama. Ain't no judge in his right mind will give you kids to raise in that run down death trap," Tigga said menacingly.

Anaya knew that he was right, so she decided not to push her luck. Since she already had her keys and purse, she stomped down the stairs and got into her car. Tears blurred her vision the entire way to her mother's house and she couldn't stop them from falling. She'd gotten so comfortable with Tigga taking care of her that she didn't know which way to turn. Rich wanted to be her man so badly, but he couldn't even afford to pay the light bill in the apartment that Tigga was leaving her in.

"I was just about to call you," Anaya's friend Erica said as soon as she got out of her truck. "Where's Amari?"

"She's at home with Tigga," Anaya replied.

"Humph," Erica frowned with an attitude.

She wasn't a big fan of Tigga's and Anaya knew that. Erica always felt that he looked down on Anaya's friends, but that couldn't have been further from the truth. Tigga was just outspoken and he always called her out when it came to Amari. He didn't care that Erica was his daughter's nanny. She didn't call the shots when it came to his daughter and he let her know it.

"Where's Rich?" Anaya questioned.

"I don't know girl. His broke ass is around here somewhere. But what's up with you? You look like you've been crying," Erica noticed.

"It's nothing. Call your cousin and tell him that I'm back here. I'm going by my mama right quick," Anaya said as she walked to her mother's trailer.

She looked around the area and wanted to cry all over again. She always felt extremely lucky that Tigga had taken her away from the run down area, but if she didn't play her hand right, she would be right back where she started from. She couldn't have that. She had shitted on too many people when she left. She always came around to show of her new clothes and anything else that Tigga had laced her with. When she got her truck, none of them bitches could tell her nothing. There was no way in hell she could come back to live there after that.

"What's wrong with you?" Donna asked when her daughter walked through her front door with a mean mug on her face.

"Nothing! Why is everybody asking me that?" Anaya snapped with an attitude.

"Oh no bitch. You will not come into my house with that attitude. You can bring your ass right back outside if it's gon' be like that," Donna fussed.

"I'm sorry ma, I just have a lot on my mind right now," Anaya apologized.

"Like what? I hope it don't have nothing to do with your broke ass ex," Donna frowned.

"Tigga broke up with me," Anaya said as a few tears escaped her eyes.

"That's what you're upset about? Tigga is always saying that he's gonna break up with you. That nigga ain't going nowhere as long as you got them babies," Donna said waving her off.

"No ma, he's serious this time. He got him another place and everything."

"What! Did he find out about...?"

"No. This has nothing to do with Rich," Anaya said cutting her mother off. "He just said that he's tired of being forced to stay with me because of the kids."

"That's bullshit! He must have another bitch out here somewhere," Donna replied.

"I don't know what to think. We're going to the vacation house next weekend and he said he's moving into his own place when we come back."

"So you're moving back in here?" Donna asked.

"No, he's paying the rent up at the apartment for six months and then I'll be on my own."

"You better put his ass on child support too. He is wrong for that shit. You better not let him see those kids either," Donna said. She did the same thing to her children's father when they were younger and it worked every time. She got her ex-husband's mind right real quick when she kept his kids away for a while.

"I probably won't have a choice. He's talking about taking me to court," Anaya revealed right as someone started knocking on the door.

Donna looked out of her side window and frowned when she saw Rich standing there. Rich was a handsome young man with light brown skin and dark brown eyes. His hair was a dirty red color but it looked good on him. Aside from that he had absolutely nothing going for himself, but Anaya couldn't seem to get enough of him.

"Go outside and talk to him. You know I don't want his thieving ass in my house," Donna spat.

Anaya ignored her mother's negative comments and went outside to talk.

"What's up baby? I tried calling you earlier," Rich said as he pulled her in for a hug.

"I couldn't talk. Tigga was home," she replied making him frown.

"Am I gonna see you this weekend? I should be able to get us a nice room for a few hours," Rich smiled while kissing her neck.

"I can't, we're going to Florida."

"Florida?" Rich questioned as he stopped his foreplay.

"Yes. Tigga wants us to take the girls to his vacation house for a few days," Anaya lied. Tigga would have loved for her stay home, but that wasn't happening.

"Why can't he take the girls and you can spend a few days with me?" Rich suggested.

"You must be crazy. I'm not letting my kids go all the way to Florida without me."

"Whatever Naya. You probably wanna go so you can be with that nigga," Rich said angrily.

"No I don't. This trip is all about my girls. We're actually going there for a reason," she replied.

"And what reason is that?" Rich questioned.

"We want to talk to the girls about us separating. We're not happy being together so I thought it was best for us to go our separate ways," Anaya lied effortlessly.

"Are you being serious right now?" Rich asked excitedly.

"Yes. I'm staying in the house with the girls and he's leaving. That's why I wanted to talk to you. It's time for you to step up your game. You claim that you want to be with me. Now is your time to prove it. This stick up kid shit ain't working so you need to find a job. A job that will support an entire family," Anaya informed him.

"I will baby. I swear I'll do whatever it takes to take care of you and the girls. You just don't know how happy I am," Rich said while bending down to kiss her.

"I am too, but don't make me regret choosing you," Anaya warned.

"I won't baby. You have my word," Rich swore as he hugged her tight.

Anaya knew that she was wrong for lying to him, but she needed to have a backup plan just in case Tigga actually went through with his decision to leave her. She was going to do everything in her power to prevent it, but she had to be prepared just in case.

"Here, I have a few dollars for you," Rich said handing her six twenty dollar bills.

It wasn't much, but it was more than she had. It was also enough for her to purchase some sexy lingerie for their trip to Florida. Once she fucked and sucked Tigga like she did when they first got together, he would more than likely change his mind before they came back home. At least that was the plan. She just hoped telling Rich what he wanted to hear didn't come back to bite her in the ass later.

Chapter 18

"I hope that's for everybody. A bitch is starving," Co-Co said when Keller walked into the shop carrying two large pizzas.

"It sure is," Keller replied as she sat the food down on her work station and went to retrieve some plates.

She had a late start because her first client, which was Tessa, wasn't coming in until one. She knew that everybody usually ate lunch around that time so she got her mother to bring her to the Italian restaurant that they frequented before bringing her to work. Mo and two of her uncles had gone with her to a car dealership early that morning, but Keller couldn't seem to make up her mind about what she wanted. Leo wanted to go, but she decided to go with her people instead. Things with the two of them were still going well with the exception of Crystal's crazy ass playing on her phone. Keller had learned her name from Leo after she threatened to leave him if he didn't tell the truth. Apparently he'd dealt with Crystal for a few months before he and Keller got back together and she just couldn't let go. Keller's feelings were kind of hurt when Leo told her that his sister was on Crystal's side. Keller and Leandra had never had any problems, so she didn't know why she would go against her like that. She even did her nails and make-up free of charge, but Leo told her that that was a wrap on that. Leandra had to pay from now on just like everybody else. Even his mother was talking in riddles. Pat just kept saying that Leo needed to be honest, but she never said about what. She told Keller that the truth was going to come out sooner or later, but she didn't know what she meant by that. Leo begged her not to let them ruin the progress that they'd made in their relationship and Keller promised him that she wouldn't.

"Did you find you a car yet?" Jaden asked as he lined up the customer that was in his chair.

"Not yet. I don't know if I want another Audi or the Lexus SUV," Kia replied.

"Get the Lexus. You already had an Audi, so go with something else," Co-Co suggested with a mouth full of pizza.

"I was thinking that too. Maybe if I test drive it I'll make my decision," Keller said.

"I can see you in a SUV. I vote for the Lexus," Candace chimed in.

"I didn't know that we were voting," Keller laughed right as the salon's front door opened. Her smile faded instantly when she saw Leandra walk into the shop with her son. She was hoping that she wasn't looking for anything free because that wasn't happening. A few seconds later another woman walked in and she too had a small little boy with her.

"Can I help y'all?" Co-Co asked once he'd swallowed his food.

"Do y'all take walk-ins?" Leandra asked loudly.

"Use your inside voice sweetie," Co-Co said as he raised his hand in the air.

"Oh, sorry," Leandra said in a lower tone.

"Now we do take walk-ins if we don't have any appointments. What is it that y'all need?" Co-Co questioned.

"I need to get my son and my nephew a haircut," Leandra replied making Keller's head snap in their direction.

Leandra had a smirk on her face, but the other woman didn't try to hide her laughter. Keller knew for a fact that Leandra didn't have a nephew. Her son was the only grandson and the others were girls. Keller was a little hurt that she walked into the shop and didn't even acknowledge her, but it was cool.

"The babies seem fine to me. I thought y'all were looking for appointments for yourselves," Co-Co pointed out.

Now it was Keller's turn to laugh, and that was exactly what she did right along with Candace. Leandra and the other woman looked at her and scowled, but she didn't turn away. They looked a hot ass mess with some cheap ass sundresses on that showed every roll on their sides and backs. Keller and Leandra had never had any problems with each other so she was surprised at her new found attitude towards her.

"I can take them before my next appointment gets here," Brian offered.

"How much does it cost?" The other woman asked him.

"You know what?" Brian asked more like a statement than a question. "You might want to take them to whoever usually cuts their hair. Ain't no five dollar haircuts up in here."

"It don't seem like y'all really want to be serviced, so what did y'all come in here for?" Co-Co inquired.

"Probably to be messy," Keller spoke up. "That's Leo's sister."

"Be messy for what? Nobody is thinking about you Keller," Leandra roared.

"Aye, y'all gotta go with all that screaming and shit," Jaden said right as he removed the cape from his customer's neck. The older man hurriedly paid for his services and rushed out of the front door.

"Come on Crystal," Leandra said pissing Keller off.

"Crystal?" Keller questioned as she stood to her feet. She couldn't believe that Leandra had the nerve to show up at her place of business with Leo's ex-bitch. The same childish bitch who had been playing on her phone for the past few months.

"Yes, Crystal, and this is my son, Leo. Oops, I meant to say Leon," she laughed like she had just told the funniest joke ever.

Keller would have loved to say that she was embarrassed, but that was a minor emotion compared to what she was feeling. It actually felt like someone had cut her heart out of her chest without using any anesthesia. She looked down at the little boy and the same face that she slept next to every night stared right back at her. There was no way in hell that Leo could tell her otherwise. That was his son and she had no doubts about that.

"Oh, my bad, I thought your man already told you about his son," Crystal said pulling Keller's gaze away from her sons'.

"I wouldn't be walking around here bragging about that shit if I were you. He's ugly just like his daddy," Co-Co said while standing to his feet.

"Fuck you!" Crystal spat angrily.

"I don't do pussy, but if I did, it damn sure wouldn't be yours," Co-Co replied.

"Don't touch me!" Leandra shouted as Co-Co pushed her and Crystal towards the front door.

"Y'all hoes about to get a beat down. Now get the fuck out and don't come back," Candace yelled as she went and stood next to her brother. Leandra and Crystal said something to her and the three of them started arguing.

"Uh-uh Candace. I know I taught you better than that. Don't ever argue with bitches who wear sundresses with dirty bra straps. Them hoes don't have nothing to live for," Co-Co said while pulling his sister away. As mad as Keller was she couldn't stop herself from laughing at that comment. Crystal and Leandra were still talking shit as they hopped in a beat down Toyota and pulled off.

"You good lil sis?" Jaden asked as he took a seat next to Keller.

"I'm hurt, but I'm good. That nigga has been lying to me for too long. I kept hearing shit about a baby, but he kept saying that people were just trying to break us up. If I never knew it before, I know without a doubt that I'm done with Leo's ass now," Keller promised.

"Good because you don't have no business being in that family anyway," Co-Co noted before he sat back down.

"Why you say that?" Candace questioned.

"Look at her," he pointed at Keller. "She is too pretty for that. Everybody in that family is ugly including the kids."

"Stop talking about people's kids. You would die if somebody talked about my two," Candace scolded.

"My niece and nephew are cute. A bitch can't say nothing about them honey," Co-Co said getting overly dramatic. He always did whenever if came to his only sister's only two kids.

"Man, these hoes been on one lately," Jaden said as he shook his head.

"You sure are right about that. It must be side bitch awareness month or something. These sideline hoes have been showing up and showing out," Co-Co agreed.

"Fuck her and Leo too," Keller said right before Tessa walked through the door for her appointment.

There was still a whole pizza left so Tessa and Keller sat down and ate before she got started on her nails. Surprisingly, Keller was in good spirits despite what had gone down just a few minutes ago. She refused to even call Leo for him to lie to her, so she just left it alone. He would know what time of day it was when he came home and saw that all of her shit was gone.

"Girl I can't wait to just chill out and relax on the beach for a few days," Tessa said as Keller started removing the polish that she'd previously had on her nails. She had three days to go before they left for their vacation and she couldn't wait.

"I know that's right. Who are you riding with?" Keller asked.

"It's just me and my mama. Tigga is trying to get us to let Naya ride with us, but that ain't happening."

"Are you taking your car?" Keller inquired.

"No, we got a rental," Tessa replied.

"You got room for one more?" Keller smirked.

"Bitch are you serious? Don't play with me Keller," Tessa yelled excitedly.

"I'm not playing. I'm coming with you. That's if your brother will let me," she replied.

"Girl you already know he'll be happy to have you. He said that you broke his heart, but he still got love for you," Tessa laughed.

"I didn't break his heart. I just stopped whatever we had before anything serious could really get started. We were both in relationships," Keller reasoned.

"He's single and ready to mingle now," Tessa said.

"Him and Anaya broke up?" Keller questioned.

"Yep. She's coming with us to Florida, but he's moving into his townhouse once we get back. All of his clothes are there already. My mama and grandma helped him decorate it."

"How is that gonna work with them going on vacation together though? Won't they have to sleep in the same room?" Keller asked.

"Tigga's place has like five or six bedrooms, so that's not an issue. Besides, Anaya and Tigga haven't slept in the same bed for months."

"Damn. Well, I might be renting a room from you when we get back," Keller revealed.

When Tessa looked at her in shock, Keller ran down everything that had happened right before she showed up. Tessa didn't seem surprised, but she was excited about having Keller staying with her for a while. Leo didn't know where she lived and he never seemed to care enough to find out. Besides, Tigga would deal with his stupid ass if he ever tried to show up to sister's house anyway.

Chapter 19

"Leo get the fuck away from my door before I send your ass to jail!" Pat yelled to her son through her locked front door. The door wasn't all that sturdy and it was bound to come down if he didn't stop kicking it.

"I ain't doing shit. Tell that bitch Crystal to come out here," Leo yelled back as he continued to bang and kick on his mother's front door.

He was livid when he got home the night before and found that Keller and all of her belongings were gone. Everything had been going good with them lately so he didn't know what prompted her sudden departure. She didn't answer the phone for him when called her all that night, but he was finally able to get through to her that morning. When she told him that his sister and Crystal had shown up at the shop with Crystal's son, he was out for blood. Keller swore that she wasn't coming back and he believed her this time. She had never taken all of her clothes before and that was how he knew that she'd always return. When she left this time she even cleared the dirty clothes hamper to make sure that she didn't leave anything.

"You need to stop disrespecting mama and leave," Leandra shouted to her brother from the huge front room window.

"Bitch you shut the fuck up. I got something for your messy ass too," Leo warned.

His anger rose to new heights when he saw Crystal standing behind his sister with a stupid looking smile on her face. They caused him to lose the love of his life and it was all a game to her. He knew that he was wrong for lying to Keller, but he didn't want her to leave him. She still ended up walking away once Leandra and Crystal got to her.

"Bitch you think this is a game? You think this shit is funny?" Leo hissed angrily.

He looked on the ground in front of his mother door and found a few small bricks underneath the stairs. They were doing construction on the house next door, so they weren't hard to find. His first mind told him to throw it through the front window, but he did something even better. When saw Crystal's raggedy Toyota parked out front, he hurled the brick through her windshield instead. It cracked, but didn't break so he kept throwing bricks until it did.

"Stop! You crazy bastard. Get away from my car," Crystal yelled as she jumped up and down like a fool. Leo didn't give a damn about how she felt. He picked up another brick and started hitting her side mirror with it.

"Leo leave that damn girl's car alone," his mother Patricia yelled to him.

"Fuck that hoe!" He replied disrespectfully.

That was nothing new to Pat. Leo was every bit of her ex-husband, from his abusive ways right on down to his disrespectful tongue. It didn't matter if she was around or not. He said whatever he wanted to say whenever he wanted to say it. Things with him only got worse once his parents got divorced and Leo went to live with his father. He picked up all of his bad habits and they were almost impossible to break now. Pat was convinced that her ex-husband hated women and her son was no different. They thought that every woman was beneath her mate and that's exactly how they treated them. Even though his father was dead and gone, his evil spirit still lived on through Leo.

"Calm down girl. That car can be replaced, but you can't," Pat said to Crystal.

She was going crazy as she watched Leo destroying what little she had left of her car. It was barley working and he was trying to finish it off. After having seen enough, she grabbed the thick piece of plywood that Pat kept behind her door and armed herself with it. Pat and Leandra screamed for her not to go outside, but she unlocked the door and ran out there anyway.

"You crazy muthafucka!" Crystal yelled as she swung the board with all her might at Leo. He jumped out of the way just in time before the wood connected with his head.

"I got you now bitch," Leo snarled while pulling the board from Crystal's hands. As soon as the weapon hit the ground he hit Crystal hard in the face with a closed fist. Crystal heard her son screaming, but she was dazed from the blow to her face. She staggered a little, but another punch to her face sent her spiraling to the ground. She was kicking and swinging trying to get Leo off of her. He had no mercy as she continued to beat her like they were equals.

"Get away from her," Leandra yelled through the opened front door. Leo ignored her as he continued to rain blows to Crystal's face and body. Her nose and lips were covered in blood, but he didn't seem to care. Pat was just standing there with the kids, but Leandra felt like she had to do something. He was going to kill her friend if she didn't. Leandra ran down the stairs and straight up to her crazy brother. He didn't even know that she was behind him until she starting punching him in his back.

"Bitch you want some too. I owe your messy ass anyway," Leo said as he turned around and pushed his sister away. He looked like the devil himself when he raised his fist into the air and came down hard, striking Leandra in her face, dropping her like a sack of potatoes. Unlike her friend, she didn't fight back because she was out cold.

"Oh hell no nigga. You don' went too far this time. Your ass is going to jail today," Pat threatened as she grabbed her phone and called the police.

"I don't give a fuck about going to jail. Do what you got to do. And make sure you have enough money to cover your bills next month too," Leo said as he calmly walked to his car and got in.

He was good about helping Pat make ends meet every month and in return she kept quiet about some of the things that he did. She could have been told Keller about his son, but she kept her mouth closed. She could have been revealed to Mo that he was using her daughter as his sparring partner too, but she remained tight lipped.

"You talking all that hot shit to me, but where are your balls whenever Mo is around. You tuck your tail and run like a lil bitch," Pat yelled angrily right before the operator came on the line. She shook her head in disgust when Leo drove by with his middle finger extended out of the window at her. His disrespect knew no boundaries and Pat was fed up. After that day, her hands were washed of her oldest son and she meant that from her heart.

***

"Oh my God Kia. You got me about to pee on myself," Keller laughed at the story that her sister was telling her.

Keller always wondered what the whole lockdown thing with Jaden was, but her sister had just enlightened her. Kia was always trying to play catch back with Jaden and was always getting busted. Keller was crying when her sister told her about what he did to her in the shower. Now she knew why Kia was blaming Jaden for her being sick.

"His ass is crazy," Kia said laughing along with her sister.

"Who thinks of shit like that?" Keller inquired.

"That's the same thing I said," Kia shook her head.

"Girl that was my laugh for the day," Keller giggled.

"I'm happy that I could help in spite of everything that's been going on. How have you been holding up?" Kia asked.

"Honestly Kia, I feel numb. Like I don't even have any more tears left to cry. Between the cheating and the beatings, I just need a break from it all," Keller replied.

"Do you need a little break or are you really done this time?"

"I need a permanent break. There is no more reconciliation," Keller swore.

"I feel you sis. I be feeling the same way sometimes. It's like I want to leave and never look back. I love Jaden, but sometimes I want to just pack up all my shit and go," Kia replied.

"My situation is different though Kia. You have Jaylynn to worry about. She loves her daddy to the moon and back. It's gonna be hard for you to do anything without him finding out."

Kia knew that her sister was right. She tried packing up and leaving Jaden once before, but that didn't work out. One call from Jaylynn and he was knocking at their door two days later. There was no way that Kia could go anywhere without her daughter ratting her out. It wasn't intentional. Jaylynn just had a strong bond with her father and she loved to be around him.

"I know, but enough about that. Are you excited about going to Florida today?" Kia asked her.

"Hell yeah," Keller smiled excitedly. "I wish Tessa hurry the hell up."

Tessa and her mother were getting the rental car and then they were picking Keller up right after. She was too excited to be getting away for a few days, especially after everything that happened between her and Leo. He had been blowing Keller's phone up like crazy, but she had no words for him. All of her belongings were already neatly situated at Tessa's house, but she wanted to chill with Kia for a little while before she left.

"Are you and your boo sleeping in the same room?" Kia said teasing her about Tigga.

"That is not my boo. And his girlfriend is coming with us anyway," Keller blushed.

"Don't try to play me heifer. Jaden said that he broke up with his girlfriend and got his own place."

"Jaden talks too damn much," Keller laughed.

"You know he came over here with Dominic and David a few weeks ago. He is too handsome," Kia complimented.

"We've been talking again for the past two days, but I don't want to rush anything. We both just got out of relationships, so I think we should take it slow."

"I agree," Kia nodded right as Keller's phone started ringing.

"This same number has been calling me since about five this morning. I wonder who it is," Keller said looking at her sister.

"Put it on speaker and let me answer, just in case it's somebody that you don't wanna talk to," Kia suggested.

Keller nodded her head and did what her sister told her to do. When Kia answered Keller cringed when she heard Leo's voice. He didn't even realize that it was Kia who answered the phone before he started talking.

"Baby I really need your help right now. I only have five minutes to use the phone," Leo spoke quickly.

"What do you want Leo?" Keller asked in an aggravated tone.

"Pat got me locked up. I need you to go to the house and get some money from the safe to bail me out," Leo answered.

"There are two problems with your request," Keller replied. "I no longer have a key to your house and I don't know the combination to the safe if I did."

"I'll give you the combination and my brother has a spare key. He can bring it to you."

"Oh, so now I can have the combination to the safe? You never wanted me to have it before."

"Don't be like that baby. I really need you. I know that we're not in a good place right now, but I promise I'll make it up to you," Leo swore.

"Your promises don't mean shit to me. I'm sorry Leo, but I can't help you. Ask Jamal to do it for you," Keller replied referring to his younger brother.

"You know I don't trust that nigga like that. Just do this one lil favor for me Keller," he pleaded.

"You better ask your baby mama to do it. My answer is no."

"I don't have a baby mama. I don't even know why you're believing that dumb shit that they told you. Keller please, I really need you right now. I don't have nobody else to handle this for me," Leo said sounding as desperate as he felt.

"Okay Leo, just stop whining. What's the code to the safe," Keller asked him. She listened as he called out some numbers, but she didn't write them down.

"I'll tell my brother to meet you at the house. I love you baby," Leo said happily.

"Okay," Keller dryly.

"I know damn well you're not going to bail his ass out of jail," Kia said right as someone started blowing their horn in front of her door.

"That's my ride boo. It's time for me to go have some fun in the sun. Fuck Leo," Keller said while jumping up from the sofa and grabbing her luggage. She gave Kia a tight hug and hurried down the stairs to Tessa's rental car.

"Have fun and call me when you make it. Love you," Kia yelled after.

"I will, love you too," Keller yelled back right before they pulled off.

Leo could rot in the prison cell for all she cared. She didn't even bother writing down the combination to his safe because she had no intentions of going to bail him out. He wasn't her problem anymore. Keller was happy to be getting away for a while, but she was even happier that she would be spending some time with Tigga. Although he and Anaya had broken up recently, Keller still didn't want to come off as being disrespectful. She had never been around Anaya for more than a few hours at a time, but she didn't have a problem being around her now. Keller had already made up in her mind that she would stay her distance from Tigga unless he came around her first. She was Tessa's guest, but she would have eyes on her brother throughout the entire trip.

Chapter 20

As much as Anaya loved coming to Tigga's vacation house in the past, she dreaded being there with him and his family now. The four hour drive from New Orleans to Destin was just awful. Tigga basically ignored her and only talked to their kids. When the kids went to sleep, he turned up his music and acted like she wasn't even there. Things only got worse when they pulled up to the gas station halfway through their trip and Tessa pulled in behind them. Anaya was livid when she saw that Tessa's uppity friend Keller was with them. She didn't really know much about Keller, but she didn't really like her. Keller acted like she was better than everyone else the few times that they were in each other's company and Anaya just couldn't get with that. It also infuriated her that Tigga didn't say more than two words to her, but he couldn't seem to shut up when he saw Keller. He was smiling in her face like she was the one who gave birth to three of his kids. When they arrived at the vacation house, he dropped their bags at the door to give Keller a grand tour of the place. Everybody was all smiles, but Anaya was ready for war.

"Is she Tessa's guest or yours?" Anaya questioned once she and Tigga were alone. Tessa, her mother and Keller had taken the kids on the strip to get ice cream while the two of them stayed behind.

"What room do you want to sleep in so I can know which one to put my stuff in?" Tigga asked ignoring her question.

"So you're sleeping in the same room with me now?" Anaya asked sounding hopeful.

"No, I just want to know where you're sleeping so I don't put my stuff in the same room," he replied shooting down all hope of them being intimate. Anaya shouldn't have been surprise since they hadn't had sex in months.

"Take whatever room you want. It's your house," Anaya snapped in irritation.

"Cool," Tigga said as he went to the smaller of the two remaining rooms. The place had five bedrooms, but Keller, Tessa and his mother had already claimed the other three. Since he was sure that his girls would probably want to sleep with their mother, he gave Anaya the room with the king size bed inside.

"So you're just gonna ignore my question?" Anaya asked as she followed behind him.

"That shouldn't be nothing new," Tigga responded.

"What shouldn't be nothing new?" Anaya questioned.

"Me ignoring you is nothing new. I'm grown. I don't have to explain anything to anybody," he shrugged nonchalantly.

"It must be true seeing as how you're not denying it."

"I already told you what the deal is with that. I don't have to say shit to you and nobody else. And we're not together anyway. Why does it matter who I'm with or what I do?"

"So you are with that bitch? Or is it somebody else? It's a reason why you wanna move out all of a sudden," Anaya said.

"All of a sudden?" Tigga questioned as he raised his voice in anger. "I was supposed to be gone three years ago, but you got pregnant with Amari. I still planned to leave, but you were sick throughout the entire pregnancy and couldn't work. You should be thanking God for our daughters because they're the only reason why I stayed as long as I did."

"Don't say I got pregnant with Amari like you weren't the one who got me pregnant," Anaya yelled.

"I took responsibility for my role in it all by staying with your ass longer than I wanted to. That's why I made sure that shit didn't happen again."

"How could it happen when you barely touch me?" Anaya yelled.

"That's why I barely touch you. I made sure to strap up every time I did though," Tigga replied.

"Once every other month ain't enough to get me pregnant anyway. And that's if I'm lucky."

"If you get it that much then you are lucky. I don't need no more 'my birth control ain't working problems'," Tigga replied sarcastically.

"Do you regret your daughter or something? Why do you always have to bring that shit up?" Anaya questioned angrily.

"Because your ass trapped me, that's why. You knew I wanted out, but you made sure I stayed just a little bit longer. I don't regret my daughter at all. I just regret that her birth forced me to be somewhere that I really didn't want to be."

"I was on birth control, but you know why they weren't effective at the time. I was on antibiotics and it weakened my birth control pills," Anaya yelled as angry tears spilled from her eyes.

Tigga was unmoved. He knew that Anaya would cry at the drop of a dime when she was called out on her bullshit. He wasn't faulting her for getting pregnant because he was just as responsible as she was. It was the timing of the pregnancy that raised the red flags for him.

"Nah, I only know what you told me. Shit sounded like a lie back then and it still sounds like a lie now," Tigga said honestly.

"Fuck you Tigga!" Anaya cried right as everyone walked back inside. They all heard the yelling in when they first walked up, but to see Anaya crying had them all wondering what had happened.

"Is everything alright?" Christy asked them both.

Anaya turned around and stormed off into the bedroom and slammed the door behind her. Thankfully the children didn't seem to notice the tension in the room as they sat down and colored in the books that their grandmother had just purchased for them.

"Hold them down for me ma. I need to go smoke," Tigga said as he walked out of the back door and onto the beach.

The vacation property was in an area that was highly frequented by tourists. It was on a strip with other vacation homes that he and the other owners rented out when they weren't occupying them. Tigga was happy that the properties close to his weren't being used so that he could have the entire back beach area all to himself. In recent years he had an enclosed hot tub installed and that was where Tessa and his mother spent most of their time. He was so stressed out that he felt like he needed to strip down and let the hot water relax him. Since he was on the beach alone, he decided to take a walk and smoke his troubles away instead.

***

"Y'all can go on ahead and go to the hot tub without me. I don't know where Tigga went off to and Anaya is sleeping," Christy said to her daughter and Keller. Tigga had been gone for over two hours, but Christy didn't want to bother him. Anaya had cried herself to sleep, so she left her alone too.

"I don't want to leave you in here with the kids when I know you really wanna get in the hot tub too," Tessa replied.

"Girl I'm fine. They've already eaten and taken their baths so I'll probably go ahead and put them to bed. And you already know how I am. If I can't sleep I'll be in the hot tub at three in the morning," Christy chuckled. Tessa laughed with her because that was true. Many mornings they woke up and found Christy in the hot tub with a good book or a glass of wine. She preferred to be in there alone anyway, so that was nothing new.

"Are you sure mama?" Tessa asked.

"I'm positive. Go show Keller why we like to come here all the time," she replied.

"Okay, I'm tired from driving anyway, so I won't be in there long. I'm going to bed early tonight. Let's go change and head downstairs Keller," Tessa said to her friend.

They both retreated to their rooms and changed into their bathing suits. Keller emerged from the room a short time later with her hot pink and orange Tory Burch halter two piece with the matching slippers. She loved the ensemble that Kia had purchased for her last birthday present. She snapped a quick selfie and sent it to her sister, letting her know that she was finally wearing it.

"You look cute," Keller complimented Tessa when she walked out wearing her all black mesh one piece bathing suit. Tessa was thick, but she was very toned and shapely.

"Thanks boo, so do you," she replied while throwing Keller one of the huge beach towels that she packed for the trip.

They both went down the back stairs and headed to the hot tub. There was another hot tub and pool that all of the guests could share, but Tessa was happy that Tigga had his own private one. She was also happy that the other properties hadn't been rented and they could have the pool all to themselves. It was a good thing that Tigga had his hot tub enclosed inside a gazebo so they didn't have to worry about seeing anyone or anyone seeing them.

"Oh my God Tessa. This water feels so good," Keller purred in satisfaction once she stepped into the oversized hot tub.

"I told you girl. Let me turn on the jets," Tessa replied while pressing a few buttons on the side of the tub.

"I swear I needed this outing and this hot tub. You can leave me here until morning," Keller said making her friend laugh.

Keller closed her eyes and relaxed her entire body. The hot water had her feeling right and she didn't ever want the moment to end. She and Tessa became lost in their own thoughts as the quietness of the small room engulfed them both. It stayed that way for over an hour until Tessa finally spoke.

"I think I've had enough. I'm going in," Tessa spoke up.

"Aww man, why? We just got in here," Keller whined.

"It's been about an hour, but that's good enough for me. I was in here falling asleep. But you don't have to rush. Stay as long as you want to," Tessa replied.

"Okay, I'll be done in a little while. It's dark and I don't want to be out here too long."

"You're fine girl. It's only four properties on this part of the beach and we're the only ones here. I might come back after I take a little nap," Tessa said.

"Okay," Keller said as she closed her eyes and drifted off into another word.

She wasn't sleepy, but she was most definitely relaxed. She texted back and forth with Kia for a while waiting for Tessa to return. When almost another hour went by, she had a feeling that her girl wasn't coming back. A call to her cell phone proved that because she was half asleep when she answered. Keller decided to call it a night and finally got out of the tub. She got excited when she heard someone pressing the keypad to gain access to the room. She thought that Tessa had changed her mind until Tigga's sexy ass walked in. Keller had to force her mouth closed when she saw him standing there shirtless with a pair of swimming trunks on. Just then she wanted to kick herself for still dealing with Leo's tall skinny ass instead of him. Tigga wasn't overly buffed, but he had a nice, toned body. Tattoos covered both of his arms, but he didn't have many on his chest and back.

"Damn," Tigga said when he saw Keller standing there in her bathing suit. "You don't have to leave because of me."

"I wasn't, I've been in here for a while. I was going back up to talk to Tessa," she replied.

"You can forget about her. I just left from up there and everybody is sleep. Well, everybody except for my mama."

"Oh," Keller replied while still walking towards the door.

"Stay and chill with me for a while," Tigga requested while lightly grabbing her arm.

"Okay," she replied without giving it a second thought.

Tigga watched as Keller lowered her sexy frame back into the water before he got in with her. He walked the beach for a few hours to clear his head and he was feeling much better. Anaya wasn't even worth the headache that she had given him earlier that day.

"I take it that you like the hot water," Tigga said when he saw Keller close her eyes and lean her head back on the side of the tub.

"Yes, I wish I could stay in here forever," Keller replied with her eyes shut tight.

"I'll make a note of that when I get ready to buy my house," Tigga replied.

"Why?" She questioned.

"Because you'll be coming to visit me," he said like that was a known fact.

Keller only smiled, but she didn't reply. She looked so pretty to him with her damp hair pulled back into a loose ponytail. The steam was rising from her skin making her look like a super model. Tigga watched her for about thirty minutes straight before he decided to walk over to her. Keller's eyes snapped open when he pulled her smaller body closer to his. Tigga saw that she was about to protest, but he covered her mouth with his before she had a chance to say anything. Keller felt weird kissing him knowing that Anaya and his family weren't too far away. She tried to break the kiss, but he wouldn't let her go. Any thoughts of stopping him vanished when Tigga picked her up and placed her on the side of the hot tub. In no time at all, he yanked off her swim suit bottoms and ran his tongue up and down her folds.

"Ooh, shit," Keller moaned softly as Tigga dipped his tongue in and out of her opening. He started out teasing her at first, but he was giving her the business soon after. Keller had her fist in her mouth trying her best to keep from being too loud. They were dead wrong for what they were doing, but it felt too good for her to stop him. Tigga was trying to mark his territory and he was doing a damn good job at it. He had Keller's legs pushed back up to her ears while he went to work on her kitty. It didn't take long before her legs started shaking and her center was crying tears of joy. Tigga seemed satisfied with his handiwork as he wiped his mouth and smiled confidently. He didn't know it, but Keller was just getting started. She wasn't like Kia when it came to oral sex. It satisfied her, but it wasn't enough. That was only foreplay as far as she was concerned. Once Keller came down from her oral high, she eased her body back into the warm water and pushed Tigga against the side of the tub.

"What you doing girl?" Tigga asked when Keller removed his boxers and trunks. He only went down on her because he didn't think that she would let him hit it. The way that she was stroking his erection let him know that she wanted it all.

"What does it look like?" Keller smirked as she wrapped her body around his and pushed his stiffness inside of her.

"Fuck!" Tigga hissed as his head fell back in pleasure. Keller was riding him nice and slow just how he liked it. He tried to remain silent, but it was almost impossible. She had him sounding like a bad R & B soundtrack, but he didn't give a damn.

"Shh," Keller said trying to get him to be quiet. She didn't know it, but Tigga hadn't had sex in a minute. She was nice and tight making his months of going without well worth it.

"Shit, wait Keller. You gotta chill ma," Tigga said when Keller started sucking on his neck right by his ear. She had found his spot without even knowing it. She was going to turn him into a five minute man if she kept doing that.

"Shut up," Keller demanded as she quickened her pace and continue to kiss and lick on his neck and ear.

She was kind of aggressive and that turned him on even more. Tigga couldn't let her punk him like that so he decided to regain control of the situation. He grabbed Keller's hips to slow her pace right before he began to drill into her at a rapid pace. The hot water from the tub was splashing all over as he pounded into Keller like a man on a mission. She had her hands wrapped snuggly around his neck while he gave her long deep strokes.

"You're gonna make me cum!" Keller screamed as Tigga hit her spot over and over again.

"That's what I'm supposed to do," Tigga replied as he kept grinding into her.

"Mmm," Keller moaned in his ear. "Don't stop. I'm cumming."

It looked like Keller was convulsing the way hers eyes rolled behind her head and her entire body shook. Tigga was almost there himself when he felt her muscles tightening around his dick like she had it in a chokehold. He wanted to keep going, but he couldn't hold out any longer. Once Keller's body stopped trembling, he pulled out of her and shot a load of semen right into the bubbling hot water.

"Fuck!" Tigga grunted loudly as he released everything that he'd been holding in for the past few months of going without. He and Keller held on to each other for a while trying to catch their breath.

"You do know that your mama is planning on coming in here sometime tonight right?" Keller asked him as she watched his babies floating around in the hot water.

"Shit, let me drain this water out right quick," Tigga said as he hopped out of the tub and put his clothes back on. Keller followed his lead and assisted him with the task. Once all of the water had run out, Tigga used some kind of spray and a brush to clean the bottom of the tub. When that was done, he used the detachable hose to wash the residue away.

"How long will it take for it to fill up?" Keller asked.

"About an hour or two," he replied while staring at her.

"What? Why are you looking at me like that?" She asked.

"Come to my room for a little while," he requested.

"You can't be serious," Keller blurted out.

"Yes I am. Why you say that?"

"Because, your girlfriend and your kids are here, that's why."

"My ex-girlfriend and my kids are asleep. It's a little after ten now, so come around eleven. I'll be done with my shower and stuff by then," he said as he kissed her lips and opened the door for her to walk out.

Keller ran back into the house and straight up the stairs to Tessa's room. Her friend was knocked out, but she really didn't care. She needed somebody to talk to and it was too late to call Kia.

"Tessa, get up," Keller said while gently shaking her arm.

"Hmm," Tessa hummed incoherently.

"Wake up, I need to talk to you," Keller begged.

"What's wrong?" Tessa mumbled.

"Everything is wrong. I'm a hoe," Keller answered.

"It's okay, most of my friends are," Tessa replied.

"Tessa I'm serious. I fucked your brother. I'm a straight up hoe and he probably thinks so too."

"Oh my God! You and Tigga slept together? When?" Tessa questioned with her eyes wide open.

"Not too long ago in the hot tub. Now he wants me to come to his room for a little while," Keller revealed.

"Are you going?" Tessa yawned.

"You think I should?" Keller asked her.

"It don't matter what I think. You and Tigga are grown. Besides, I can see it in your eyes. You're going no matter what I say," Tessa laughed.

"Do you think I'm a hoe for giving it up so fast? I hope he doesn't think so."

"Girl stop talking crazy. You are not a hoe. Tigga likes you and you like him. He wouldn't be asking you to come to his room if he thought less of you. Why does it matter how long it took y'all to have sex? Obviously he liked it and he wants some more of it," Tessa smirked.

"I'm going to bed," Keller said as she stretched and walked to the door.

"Yeah right. Y'all just keep it down so nobody will hear y'all," Tessa teased right before Keller walked out of her room.

Keller walked down the hall to her own room and stripped out of her wet bathing suit. After taking a quick shower, she threw on a pair of leggings and a tank. She laid down for a while debating if she should go to Tigga's room or not. She knew that they were playing with fire, but she was really feeling him. Not to mention their quickie in the hot tub had her feigning for more. Just when she decided that she wanted to go, the doubt started to creep in. Tigga hadn't tried to call or text, so maybe he'd changed his mind about her coming to his room. Maybe he decided to hook up with his baby mama instead. Although Keller had no right to be, she found herself getting jealous. It had been over an hour since they went their separate ways and Tigga didn't seem to be worried about her. Keller eased out of her room and down the long hall towards the room that Anaya and her kids were occupying. She didn't hear any movements or voices, but that didn't mean anything to her. Tigga and his mother's room were on the other side of the huge house along with the kitchen and sitting room. Keller tried to be as quiet as she possibly could, but obviously she wasn't quiet enough. As soon as she was passing by Tigga's room, his door flew open and he pulled her inside.

"It's about time. I was just about to come get your ass," he said as he planted a kiss on her lips. Once she was safely inside, Tigga locked the door and started stripping Keller out of her clothes. She didn't have to wonder any longer. The way that he was pulling her out of her clothes showed her that he definitely wanted her in his bed. Keller just didn't know for how long.

Chapter 21

Keller woke up a little after noon the following day. She and Tigga went at it for hours the night before and that nigga was the truth. She didn't leave until after four that morning, but it was well worth it. Leo could forget about whatever they once had because Keller damn sure did. Tigga made sure of it too with the way he worked her body out like a professional trainer. They showered together in his room and she left right after. As soon as Keller got back to her room, she was fast asleep as soon as her head hit the pillow.

"Good morning," Keller said when she entered the kitchen and saw everybody sitting around the table eating. Tigga was the only one missing, but he was probably still sleeping too. Anaya looked like she'd been sucking on a lemon with the frown that she had on her face, but Keller ignored her.

"Good afternoon," Tessa clarified with a smirk.

"Hush up. You know what I mean," Keller laughed.

"My mama cooked shrimp and grits, so help yourself," Tessa offered.

"Thanks," Keller said as she grabbed a bowl and fixed herself something to eat. She and Tessa made small talk while they ate their food. Anaya's attitude was on one hundred so they basically ignored her.

"What are you girls getting into today? I was thinking that we could go to the water park since we haven't done that in a while. You'll like that Keller," Christy said.

She smiled when her granddaughters started getting excited because she knew that they would be happy with her choice. They loved to feed the dolphins and get on the jet skis with their father. Christy only went for the seafood, but she was happy as long as her grandkids were having a good time.

"That's sounds good to me," Keller replied making Anaya suck her teeth in disgust.

"Y'all can go. I'll find something else for me and my girls to do on the strip," Anaya announced.

"Aww man. We wanna go with grandma to feed the dolphins," Tia complained to her mother.

"I don't want to go on the strip," Talia pouted.

"Y'all don't have any wants. We can find something fun to do on the strip," Anaya announced.

"If you want some alone time on the strip I can bring them with me Anaya. You know it's not a problem," Christy offered.

"I don't need no alone time. I just want to spend time with my daughters by myself," she replied smartly.

"You could have stayed your miserable ass at home if you're gonna have an attitude the whole time we're here," Tessa argued.

"Was I talking to you? You need to learn how to mind your own damn business," Anaya snapped.

"Bitch my nieces are my business," Tessa yelled while standing to her feet.

"I got your bitch," Anaya replied as she too got up from her chair.

Keller grabbed Tessa's arm to keep her from going after her niece's mother. That wouldn't have been a good look to do that in front of them.

"That's enough!" Christy yelled. "We will not do this in front of these babies."

"Don't tell me what to do, I'm grown. That's your daughter over there just in case you forgot," Anaya replied flippantly while pointing to Tessa.

"Bitch!" Tessa screamed as she tried to break free from Keller's grasp. "I'm tired of you disrespecting my mama."

"What the hell is going on in here?" Tigga's deep voice boomed when he walked into the kitchen.

He thought he was dreaming when he heard all the yelling and screaming coming from within the house. The sleep was still evident in his eyes since they woke him up from a deep slumber. When he saw Keller holding his sister back he already knew what the deal was. Tessa and Anaya were obviously at it again. They use to get along great in the beginning, but things quickly went downhill after the first year of Tigga and Anaya's relationship. He knew that Anaya's slick mouth and disrespectful attitude had a lot to do with it.

"You better get your sister. Ole lonely ass needs to find herself a man," Anaya spat angrily.

"Bitch I'm single by choice. You were forced into the single life. Desperate, broke ass hood rat," Tessa yelled.

"That's enough with the language Tessa!" Christy scolded.

"I'm sorry ma, but I'm sick of her," Tessa apologized.

"Bitch I'm sick of you too. How you get mad because I want to spend time with my own damn kids?" Anaya questioned.

Tessa was about to reply until Keller pulled her away to another room. Tigga was happy for that because they were giving him a headache.

"Y'all go outside on the beach with grandma while me and your mama talk,"Tigga told his daughters.

Christy ushered her granddaughters outside, leaving their parents alone to talk.

"What happened?" He asked Anaya.

"First of all, I was talking to your mama. Tessa didn't have shit to do with it. Christy wanted to do watersports today, but I told her that me and the girls will find something to do on the strip instead," Anaya replied making Tigga mad without even knowing it.

"But why when you know they like to do the watersports?" He asked.

"Okay, but I want to spend time with my own kids. Is that a problem?"

"It is if you don't have any money to do shit with them," Tigga replied.

"So you wouldn't even give me money to spend time with your own kids. That's fucked up," Anaya said shaking her head.

"Nah, what's fucked up is you being so childish. That's exactly why I didn't want you to come. You barely spend time with them at home. Now you want to act like it's a matter of life or death for you to spend time with them now. It's like you do shit just to get under people's skin. And just so you know, finances are never a problem for my kids."

"Okay, so that means that you're going to give me some money to do something with them right?" Anaya questioned.

"Yeah, just as long as its watersports. If you don't want to do that then you can stay inside and let my mama take them. You can be miserable all you want to, but you not about to make my girls miserable with you," Tigga said right before he walked off and went into the bathroom.

After arguing with Anaya the night before, he didn't get a chance to do anything with his daughters. Going with them to the Watersports Park would give him a chance to spend some time with them. He wanted to sleep in a little later, but their loud arguing prevented him from doing that. He was tired as hell from staying up all night with Keller, not that he was complaining. She kept saying that they were moving too fast, but he wasn't trying to hear that. He wanted her and he wasn't going to stop until he got her. Their chemistry was great and the sex was even better. That was hard to find and he wasn't ready to let it go. Tigga completed his morning hygiene and helped himself to the breakfast that his mother had cooked. Tessa and Keller were still locked up in the room, so he headed outside to the beach to chill with Christy and his girls.

"Tigga," Amari yelled as she ran up to him with her arms out for him to hold her.

"What did I tell you about that?" He scolded his two year old little busy body. "What's my name?"

"Daddy," Amari replied with a smile when he picked her up. She was too smart and knew exactly what she was doing. She always said mommy and daddy when she wanted something, but it was Tigga and Naya any other time.

"Is everything alright up in there?" Christy asked her son.

"Yeah, it's cool. We can get ready to go to the water park whenever y'all get ready," Tigga replied.

"Amari go play with your sisters," Christy instructed her granddaughter. She watched as Amari climbed off of her father's lap and ran over to play in the sand with the other girls.

"What's up?" Tigga asked knowing that his mother had something to say.

"I'm not about to sit here and lie or pretend that Anaya is one of my favorite people. You and I both know that she's not. I'm actually happy that you'll be in your own place when we get back home," Christy revealed.

"But?" Tigga questioned knowing that his mother had more to say.

"But she is the mother of your kids and she is here with us, even though I wish that she wasn't. You can do whatever you want once we get back to New Orleans, but just be respectful while we're here," Christy replied.

"What are you talking about?" Tigga asked.

"I saw Keller coming out of your room early this morning," Christy reveled.

"Okay," Tigga said like it was no big deal.

"Now I don't know what's going on or for how long and it's really none of my business. Keller is a beautiful girl and I can see why you're interested in her, but I don't want any drama while we're out here. If y'all want to pursue a relationship once we get back home that's fine. I just want you to be mindful of what you're doing while we're here. She needs to stay out of your room and I mean it," Christy replied.

"You got that ma," Tigga said just to be done with the conversation.

He loved his mother, but he had no intentions of honoring her wishes. Keller had him hooked after just one night and he wasn't ashamed to admit it. Christy said that Keller needed to stay out of his room, but she never said anything about him going to hers.

***

"Are you okay now Mayweather?" Keller joked with Tessa.

"I'm fine girl. I'm not letting Anaya ruin my vacation," Tessa replied.

"I know that's right. But I've been meaning to ask you something. If I'm getting too personal just let me know."

"You're my best friend Keller. You can ask me anything."

"I know that you said your grandpa got this house for Tigga, but what about you? I know he's the only grandson, but don't you feel left out sometimes?" Keller asked.

"Not at all. You see that big tan colored house next door?" Tessa questioned.

"Yeah," Keller replied.

"That use to be mine."

"Are you serious?" Keller asked in shock.

"Yep. My grandpa got it for me the same time he got this one for Tigga, but he sold mine. I told you that I was in a toxic relationship for a while. That's why I'm single and only date when I want to. I was so stupid for my ex that my grandpa cut me off for a long time. That nigga didn't work, but he was living damn good off of me. I owned a portion of the company, but I lost that too. I was making stupid decisions and my grandpa got tired of me letting a man control what I did. He went through enough with my daddy and he said he wasn't doing it with me too."

"But you weren't on drugs like you father, were you?" Keller asked.

"No, but my ex was. He was in my bank account so much that my grandma had to put a freeze on it. Thank God he did or I would have been flat broke. He started stealing from me and getting credit from the dealers after that. It got so bad that people started coming to my house looking for him. The last straw was when my door got kicked in because he owed a big time drug dealer some money. That's how I ended up going to school out of town. My grandpa didn't want me to get killed over his bullshit."

"Damn. Whatever happened to your ex?" Keller questioned.

"Died from a drug overdose," Tessa said right before she walked out of the room.

Now Keller understood why Tessa just up and moved out of town to go to school. She had only known her for a short period of time then, but she didn't know much about her ex. Keller thought that he might have been abusive because Tessa would get nervous every time he called. She understood why Tessa wasn't in a rush to jump into another relationship. After going through something like that she didn't blame her. After years of going through ups and downs with Leo, Keller was surprised that she was thinking about being in another relationship so soon. She couldn't help it though. Tigga seemed so different than any man that she'd ever been with. Granted, she'd only been with two men, but she hoped that the third time was the charm.

Chapter 22

"Dam girl," Leo moaned as he watched his dick disappear down Erica's throat.

She was sucking like her life depended on it, but he really wasn't into it like he should have been. Erica was one of his side chicks that he dealt with from time to time when Keller was on her bullshit. He met her through her cousin Rich, who he met when he was locked up once. He used Rich to do some of his dirty work from time to time, but that was about it. Leo tried to put Rich on to make some money with him, but it just wasn't in his blood. Rich was a jack boy, but he wasn't even good at that. Leo let him make drops for him every now and then just to keep money in his pockets. His cousin Erica was cool for sex, but that was about it. She had a few kids and that was a turn off for Leo. Living in a run-down trailer park was not what he envisioned for a woman that he wanted to be with. Besides, Erica and any other woman that he was with only served as a distraction when Keller wasn't around. She was the only woman who he wanted to be with. She had his heart in the palm of her hands. He knew that he was pushing her away with his erratic behavior and he promised himself that he was going to do better. He knew that Keller was fed up anytime she left him in jail without bothering to get him out. He was furious at first, but he calmed down once he thought things through. Keller had just found out about him having a son, so that was a lot to take in. She was probably making him suffer for lying about it all that time. She swore that she was coming to get him, but she never made good on her promise. After spending three nights behind bars, Leo had to beg and plead with Erica to get a loan just to bail him out. He paid back every penny of the loan when he was released and he appreciated her being there for him. She even waited outside of the prison until he was released. Erica was pissed because the first thing he did when he did get out was go straight to the shop to look for Keller. He even sent her inside to see if she was in there because he didn't want to run into Jaden. He was sure that Keller had told him and her sister what was going on and he wasn't in the mood to deal with it. When Erica came back and told him that Keller was on vacation he didn't know which way to turn. Neither Kia nor Mo liked him enough to give him any info and he didn't know Tessa's number or where she lived. He decided to give it some time and wait for her to return.

"Get me a towel and go wash yourself up," Leo frowned once he came all over Erica's face and neck.

He tried to drop his load in the towel that was on her floor, but she had other plans. She liked that nasty shit, which was another reason that he didn't want to be with her. With his babies dripping down her chin, Erica retreated to the bathroom to do what he told her to do. She came back a few minutes later with a clean face and soapy towel in her hand. She tried to clean him up, but Leo snatched the towel from her and did it himself.

"You want something to eat?" Erica asked, trying to get him to stay longer. Usually Leo would be fucking her brains out by now, but she was on her cycle.

"Nah, I'm about to get going. I need to see if Keller went back to work yet," he replied while fixing his clothes.

"I don't know why you're still chasing after her. She's obviously not worried about you. She wouldn't have left you in jail if she was," Erica spat angrily.

"Stay the fuck out of my business. Whatever happens with me and Keller don't have shit to do with you."

"I'm just tired of you constantly shittin' on me for Keller when I'm the one that's always here for you. I'm not beneath her and you need to stop making me feel like I am," Erica said.

"I'm not making you feel like nothing. You already know what it is. You got three babies with three baby daddies, but you want a nigga to treat you like a queen. You live in a fucking trailer that your mama died and left you. You don't even keep this bitch clean," Leo said turning his nose up in disgust.

"What does the condition of my house have to do with anything?" Erica said sounding stupid.

"It has everything to do with it. Every time me and Keller break up you always beg me to be with you, but you don't even handle your business. Every time I come here your house and your kids are a fucking mess. What I look like leaving my girl alone for good to come to this shit? You don't have a job or nothing else going for yourself. Being a freak ain't enough."

"It's not like I'm getting a prize with you either," Erica pointed out.

Leo had confidence through the roof to say he wasn't the best looking man that she'd ever been with. His swag was on one thousand, but his face was nothing to brag about. He could dress his ass off and she was sure that other females noticed him because of that.

"You talk a lot of shit for a bitch who still got my dried up cum in her hair," Leo laughed sarcastically as he walked to the door.

"I don't see what's so funny. You're gonna need me one day and I won't be here when you do." Erica swore.

"You ain't going nowhere. But I got a few other bitches on my team just in case you do," he shrugged uncaringly and walked out of her front door.

He dialed his brother's number as soon as he got into his car and pulled off.

"Yeah," his brother Jamal said when he answered the phone.

"Did you get your girl to do it?" Leo asked.

"Yeah," Jamal drawled.

"What happened?" Leo questioned.

"Keller's back, but she wasn't there when she called," Jamal answered.

"Alright, cool. Tell your girl that I said thanks," Leo said before hanging up the phone.

He'd been having his little brother's girlfriend calling the shop every day for the past few days asking for Keller. She hadn't been answering his calls, so he knew that she was still mad with him. He was excited to know that she'd finally made it back from wherever she had gone off too. Leo was curious as to where she had been, but he was just happy that she had returned. It was time for him to get his girl back and make things right. He knew that a lot of niggas would have been happy to have Keller on their arm and he couldn't have that. Keller was his heart and he would die before he let another man have what was his.

***

"Shit baby, I'm about to cum." Tigga yelled right as he pulled out and came all over Keller's round ass. They both collapsed on the bed, drenched in sweat.

"We have to stop this. I was supposed to be back at work days ago," Keller panted.

They had come back from Florida three days ago and she'd been relaxing at Tigga's house since they returned. He hadn't had a chance to enjoy his own place because Keller had been their every day. It was his idea, so he really didn't mind.

"We ain't stopping shit. I'm paying you for my time," Tigga chuckled.

"I told you to stop saying that. You make it seem like I'm a prostitute," Keller fussed.

"Get out your feelings. I'm just fucking with you. But seriously, you know I got you if you need anything. I know that you're missing out on money by being here with me," Tigga replied.

"It's not just about the money. I don't like disappointing my customers."

"Didn't you refer them to somebody else until you come back?" Tigga questioned.

"Yeah, I did," she replied.

Shanti was a girl that Keller graduated from cosmetology school with. She was a pretty decent nail tech who worked in a salon a few blocks away from Bryce's shop. Whenever either one of them were unavailable they referred their customers to each other.

"What's wrong?" Tigga asked when he saw her trying to reach around him to grab something.

"I'm trying to get my phone. I need to know what time it is," Keller replied.

"You sure that's the only reason why you want your phone?" Tigga asked with raised brows. Leo had been blowing Keller's phone up like crazy, but she never answered for him.

"Don't start Tigga. I don't say nothing when Anaya calls your phone all day and night," Keller replied.

Anaya had become a straight up pain in the ass since they got back from Florida. She called all day and night claiming that the girls wanted to talk to him. Most of the time it sounded like they were sleeping when they got on the phone. If it wasn't that she was calling to ask for stuff that they probably didn't even need. Tigga tried his best to handle things the right way. He sat down and explained to his daughters about their new living arrangements as best as he could. They were young, but they were also very smart. Their first day back home, Tigga had taken them to his new place to show them were he would be living. They were excited to know that they would have two rooms at two different houses. He made sure to let them know that they could come to his house to sleep or visit any time they wanted to. Things went over smoothly with them, but Anaya was another story.

"You know I don't want no damn Anaya," Tigga said after a long pause.

"And you know I don't want no damn Leo," Keller countered.

"You're not starting to have doubts again are you?" Tigga asked just to be sure.

"No, we talked about this already. If there were any doubts I wouldn't have taken it to the next level with you. I wouldn't even be here right now," Keller said honestly.

"I'm just making sure. I don't want to put myself in a position to get my feelings hurt."

"I'm putting myself in the same position. Both of us are just coming out of a relationship. That's why I told you that we need to take it slow," Keller replied.

"You should have said that before you gave me the pussy. It's too late for taking things slow now," Tigga said seriously.

"I can't with you," Keller laughed as she got up from the bed.

"Where you going?" He asked her.

"You know I have be at the dealership at four. My mama is coming to get me. I won't be that long. The paperwork is already done. I just have to pick up the car," Keller replied.

She'd finally decided to go with the Lexus truck, but they had to order the color that she wanted. She paid more to get the truck in bronze, but it was well worth it.

"I could have taken you to do that. You want me to come with you?" Tigga offered.

"I did say that my mama is coming with me," Keller answered.

"It's cool if you're not ready for me to meet her yet, but she's going to wonder whose house this is that she's picking you up from," Tigga answered.

"It's not that I don't want you to meet her. Mo just has a way of seeing things differently. It was like Kia and I never could hide anything from her. She saw right through us every time. She hates Leo, but I really want her to like you."

"Why wouldn't she like me?" Tigga questioned.

"I don't know, but I think I better let her pick me up from Tessa's house," Keller suggested.

"Hell no Keller. We're not even about to start that shit. I'm a grown ass man. I'm not hiding from your mama and nobody else," Tigga argued.

"But...," Keller started before he cut her off.

"But nothing. I'm not starting our relationship off like that. That shit is childish as fuck," Tigga frowned.

"So we're in a relationship now?" Keller blushed.

"Girl stop acting like you don't want to be with a nigga," Tigga laughed.

"Okay, but don't say that I didn't warn you about Mo. She gon' get all in your business and ask you a thousand questions."

"I don't have nothing to hide. I'll tell her whatever she wants to know. I might even tell her that her daughter is a freak," he teased as she chased her into the bathroom.

He and Keller took a quick shower together before getting dressed. Tigga wanted to drive her to Mo's house, but Keller called her mother to pick them up instead. She was a little nervous about Mo meeting him. Tigga was one of the good ones, but Mo was going to pick him apart. She did that with everything that involved her daughters. She even gave the people at the dealership a hard time about Keller's car. It worked out fine thought because she got the car that she wanted.

"Please don't take nothing that my mama says personal. I hide a lot of stuff from her because she's so overprotective," Keller said when Mo called to tell her that she was outside.

"Calm your paranoid ass down. I'm not scared of your mama," Tigga said right before they walked outside.

Mo was standing outside of the car looking like a slightly older version of Keller and her sister. She looked so sweet and innocent, but Tigga was no fool. Her daughter had told him some stories about her and believed every one of them. Jaden had already told him that Mo didn't play behind her only two girls.

"Hey baby," Mo said giving Keller a tight hug.

"Hey Ma. This is Tyler," Keller said introducing Tigga by his real name.

"How you doing ma'am?" Tigga said as he stepped up shook Mo's hand.

"Monique or Mo is fine. Do you prefer to be called Tyler or Tigga?" She asked him.

"You can call me Tigga," he replied with a smile.

Keller gave her mother a strange look, wondering how she knew about his nickname.

"Stop looking at me like that girl," Mo laughed. "I got my ways of knowing what I need to know. He's Tessa's brother right?"

"Yeah," Keller replied in shock. "How do you know that?"

"I got my ways," Mo smiled at her. Kia was so excited that Keller was dating someone other than Leo. She told Mo all about Tigga and what he did for a living. Kia seemed to think that he was good for her sister and Mo had to agree. She asked around about him and no one had a bad word to say. His father was a known junkie in the hood, but that didn't have anything to do with is son. She knew all about Tigga's baby mama too. Mo knew that Anaya had the potential to be a problem for her daughter, but she would deal with that issue if it were to ever become one.

"I guess we need to get going," Keller said after a few minutes of lingering silence.

"Wait, I left my phone. I'll be right back," Tigga said as he jogged up the steps and back into the house.

"So," Keller said looking at Mo. "What do you think?"

"I think he's very handsome."

"And?" Keller pressed her mother to say more.

"And I think you really like him," Mo answered.

"I do," Keller admitted.

"So do I," Mo winked.

"So, you don't think we're moving too fast?" Keller asked her mother.

"You're asking that question to a woman who was pregnant when she went in to get her six week checkup," Mo said making her daughter laugh.

"Say no more," Keller said as she got into her mother's car.

As soon as Tigga came out they were on their way to the car dealership. Keller was beaming from ear to ear. She didn't know what made her happier. The fact that she was minutes away from having her own car again or maybe it was Mo giving her the green light on her relationship with Tigga. Either way it went she had a whole lot to smile about.

Chapter 23

"I'm not doing this shit with you no more Anaya," Rich yelled as he jumped up from the bed and started to get dressed. They were at his cousin Erica's house occupying one of her bedrooms once again. Erica lived in a three bedroom trailer, but she also had three kids that lived there with her. Rich always had to put Erica's kids in one room so that he and Anaya could have some privacy. Erica was out doing God knows what so they had to babysit until she came back.

"I'm not doing this with you either. We argue about the same shit every day," Anaya snapped while pulling her shirt over her head.

"That's because you're fucking a liar. You fed me all that bullshit about us being together, but you didn't mean none of it. We're still sneaking around like kids and you and that nigga ain't even together no more. You got the house to yourself, but we're still fucking in Erica's trailer."

"And I already told you why," Anaya yelled.

"You said that you weren't ready to bring anyone around your kids. I understand that, but they're not even home right now," Rich ranted

"It's not that easy Rich. Tigga still pays all of the bills. If he finds out I got another nigga sleeping in the house that he pays for he's going to go off. Can you afford to keep a roof over our heads? You couldn't even afford to get us a room for the night. That's the reason we came here to begin with."

"That's bullshit. You always throwing money in my face trying to prove your point, but I'm not buying it this time. That nigga don't give a fuck about what you do or who you do it with. I'm really starting to believe that he's the one who broke up with you instead of the other way around. From what I'm hearing he's already moved on," Rich said crushing Anaya's sprits.

Truth be told, Anaya had heard the exact same thing from her own mama. Donna saw Tigga out eating with another woman one night. She made sure to call her daughter and let her know every little detail of what she saw. In her mind she was right and that was why Tigga broke up with Anaya in the first place. Anaya tried to get information from her daughters, but they really didn't know anything. They swore that it was just their father at the house whenever they went over there.

"I'm with you now, so I don't care if he did move on," Anaya said after a long awkward pause.

"Miss me with that sweet talking shit. I can't keep doing this."

"Don't be like that baby. It's only been a month since Tigga and I have been broken up. Just give me some time to get my girls adjusted to the situation," Anaya begged.

"You're talking about the past month. I'm talking about the past few years. I feel like less than a fucking man to even let this shit go on as long as it did. I've kept your secrets and pretended to be unaffected when all awhile that shit has been tearing me up inside. I knew I couldn't provide the kind of life that y'all deserved and that's the only reason why I fell back," Rich said as his eyes filled up with liquid pain.

Anaya lowered her head in shame. She was so busy trying to keep Tigga and make him happy that she never thought about how her actions were affecting Rich. Tigga had introduced her to the good life and she didn't want to give that up for anybody. Things still went left because Tigga didn't even want to be with her anymore. And just like always, Rich was there to pick up the pieces of her broken heart. Anaya knew that he was getting tired and he didn't blame him. He really did deserve more than what she was giving him.

"Baby," Anaya said as she wrapped her arms around Rich's slender body. "I'm sorry."

"No Anaya," he said as he pushed her away. "Don't try to tell me what you think I want to hear. If you don't mean what you say then just shut up."

"I do mean it. I'm sorry and I promise to make things right."

"There's only one way that you can make things right. If you're not willing to be completely honest then just leave me alone. I'm not being nobody's side nigga no more," Rich said seriously.

"I'll be honest. I'll let Tigga know about you and our relationship. Just give me time Rich. I'm not asking for more years. Just a few more weeks," Anaya begged.

"Okay, but if you're lying to me I'm done with you for good and I mean that," Rich swore.

"You have my word," Anaya said as she raised her right hand in the air like she was being sworn in.

She smiled inside when she saw that Rich was giving into her just like he always did. She knew that he was getting tired of being kept in the dark, but things weren't as easy as they seemed. Rich was still rubbing pennies together trying to make ends meet and Anaya just couldn't trust him to provide for her. His criminal background prevented him from getting a decent job and his illegal activities didn't pay very much. She just needed to stall him for a while longer to see if things with her and Tigga were really over. If there was any chance at all of them getting back together then it was a wrap with her and Rich. The first thing Anaya had to do was find out who the mystery woman was that he'd been seeing. She needed to know who her competition was so that she could eliminate her and get her man back.

***

"The fuck did you get this raggedy ass car from?" Leo asked Rich.

They were parked outside of Keller's job waiting for her to come out. He didn't want to take his car so he jumped on it when Rich offered to pick him up. He didn't know that they were going in two-toned piece of shit that sounded like a tow truck.

"Some crack head that lives in the trailer park," Rich chuckled.

"Nigga you ain't tired of living in that damn trailer park?" Leo asked.

"What you think?" Rich said looking at him like he was crazy. "I'm trying to get my money up, but the shit is just hard. You need to put your boy on."

"I can't do nothing for you fam. I ain't never seen a nigga who can't even sell a few bags of weed," Leo said shaking his head.

Rich had Leo fooled when they were locked up together. He made it seem like he was out there doing his thing before he went to jail. Once Leo was released it didn't take him long to find out that Rich was a liar. Not only was the nigga broke, but he lived with his mama and the rest of his siblings in a trailer. Leo barely made enough money to keep clean clothes on his ass.

"Man, I already told you that dope ain't my thing. I'll take a nigga's dope money, but I can't do no selling."

"You can't even do that right. Robbing them lil corner boys ain't getting you nothing."

"I need to do something man. My girl is getting tired of me being broke," Rich sighed.

"Your girl? You talking bout that money hungry bitch that you be creepin' with?" Leo asked.

"She ain't money hungry, but she got bills," Rich said defending Anaya.

"That bitch ain't right bruh. You a better man than me though. That hoe could have never played me how she played you all this time. And you letting her do the shit is what got me confused," Leo said shaking his head.

"We talked about that the other day. Everything is all good now."

"So her ex nigga know what's up with y'all?" Leo questioned skeptically.

"Not yet, but she's gonna tell him what the deal is," Rich said confidently.

"I need to meet this bitch. Either she got that fire between her legs or she got one hell of a mouth piece. She got you believing shit that don't even make sense," Leo said laughing.

"It's not like that man. Sometimes you do stupid shit when you love a person. Like right now. We're out here stalking your ex who don't want you no more. If that ain't love I don't know what is," Rich chuckled.

"Nah, this ain't nothing like what you got going on. This bitch is playing with my emotions for real," Leo replied in anger.

It had been over a month and Keller was still refusing to talk to him. She answered for him one time and told him that they were really over, but Leo just couldn't accept that. He knew without a doubt that she meant it that time though. He was shocked when he offered to pick her up from work one day and she told him that she had her own vehicle. She was really trying to show him that she didn't need or want anything from him. He saw her getting into her truck one day outside of the shop and he was impressed with her choice. Keller claimed that she was living with Kia, but he didn't believe her. A few times when he passed in front of Kia's house he didn't see her truck anywhere, so that had to be a lie. He tried following her twice before, but he quickly went his own way when he saw that she was headed straight to Mo's house. He'd been trying to catch her for a few days to see where she was going, but his schedule didn't always allow him to. He made it his business to free up his schedule that particular day to see exactly what she was up to. It didn't matter if he got turned down by other women, but that was unacceptable when it came to Keller.

"Maybe it's really a wrap on y'all being together this time," Rich said pulling Leo away from his thoughts.

"Nigga you sound stupid. It ain't never a wrap on that. Keller's ass is just spoiled. She like it when a nigga kiss her ass and chase after her. This ain't the first time I fucked up and I'm sure it won't be the last," Leo noted.

"Yeah, but there was never a baby involved before. Your sister and her girl did you dirty with that shit."

"And that's why I tried to murder both of them bitches with my bare hands," Leo frowned.

"You still ain't talk to your mama since you got out?" Rich questioned.

"I don't have shit to say to her either. She's on Leandra's side, so fuck her too," Leo spat.

"Damn bruh, your mama though?" Rich said shaking his head.

"Mama or not, she can get it too. Pat ain't do shit for me. My pops raised me up until the day he took his last breath. She's lucky that I helped her ass out as much as I did. Bitch got a restraining order on me, so she's on her own now," Leo replied.

"You ain't got no heart to say some shit like that about your own mama," Rich frowned.

I got a heart and that's the bitch who's trying to break it," Leo said as he pointed at Keller who was walking out of the shop with Jaden. Her bother-in-law made sure she got into the truck and pulled off before going back inside.

"Damn," Rich said when he looked over at her.

"Don't put your mama through the pain of having to bury one of her kids. Keep your eyes on the road and off of my bitch," Leo threatened.

"Damn bruh, she got you gone like that?" Rich chuckled.

"Just drive nigga," Leo ordered.

Doing as he was told, Rich pulled out of the parking lot and followed behind Keller's Lexus truck. Leo looked anxious sitting in the passenger's seat, but he didn't know why. He'd been knowing Leo for at least three years, but he'd never met Keller before. That night was his first time actually laying eyes on her. Leo and his cousin Erica messed around from time to time, but he'd never seen him act like that over her. He didn't seem to have feeling for Erica at all outside of the bedroom. Rich could tell that Leo really loved Keller and that was proven by what they were doing. He'd never followed a woman a day in his life. As much as he loved Anaya, he'd never tried to follow her before. He was tempted a few times just so he could see what Tigga looked like. Anaya was so in love with the nigga that Rich just wanted to see what all the fuss was about. Aside from a few pictures on her phone he never got a chance to lay eyes on him. It was crazy because he knew so much about a man who didn't even know that he existed.

"Pull to the side," Leo said pulling Rich back to the present.

They parked at the curb across the street from a Chinese restaurant that Keller had just gone into. About ten minutes later, she came back out carrying a large brown bag full of food.

"I'm a kill that bitch!" Leo yelled out in frustration.

"For what? Eating?" Rich questioned.

"For playing these hoe ass games. She use to stop here at least twice a week to get us food before she came home from work. I guarantee you she's going by a nigga," Leo answered.

"Only one way to find out," Rich said as he continued his pursuit.

They continued to follow Keller as she got up on the bridge and headed towards Metairie. The route was unfamiliar to Leo and he knew that Kia nor Mo lived in the area. He prayed that it was Tessa's house that she was going to, but his gut was telling his otherwise.

"Fuck!" Leo yelled when Keller pulled up to a gated area that housed a bunch of townhouses. There was a guard at the gate who went up to Keller's truck as soon as she pulled in. They seemed to be familiar just by the way they were talking and laughing with each other.

"Now what?" Rich asked him.

"Just pull off man. Best believe I'll be back around this bitch soon though. I need to know exactly who the fuck lives back here," Leo said angrily.

He didn't know how long it would take, but he was going to find out what was up with Keller sooner or later. Some shit just wasn't adding up and he was determined to get to the bottom of it. He still had an open case thanks to his mama, so he had to watch how he moved. He was praying that his probation officer didn't violate him because he couldn't do anything from behind bars. Leo sat deep in thought as Rich pulled away from the curb and headed in the direction that they had just come from.

***

"If you don't feel comfortable I can pick you up and drop you off to work," Tigga said as he and Keller ate the Chinese food that she had just picked up.

"No, I had enough of that with Leo. It feels good to have my own car again," Keller replied.

"I don't want you to be scared though baby. If it'll make you feel better you can drop me off to and from work so you don't have to ride by yourself."

"You are too sweet," Keller smiled at him. "I'm okay. I just felt kind of weird when I left work today."

"Weird like what?" Tigga inquired.

"I don't know. Leo kept calling me all day. I blocked his number, but he started calling from other phones. For some reason I just expected him to be outside of the shop waiting for me when I got off."

"Jaden has been walking you out though right?" Tigga asked.

"Yeah, he walks me out and makes sure I get in my car safely," she replied.

"That's good, but do you think you might need some protection?" Tigga questioned.

"You mean like a gun?"

"Yeah. You can get certified to carry. You can even go to the range to learn how to shoot. Put that nigga on some papers and light his ass up if he comes too close to you."

"You sound just like Kia. She was talking about doing the same thing with that crazy girl Tori," Keller laughed.

"Maybe y'all can go together. You might feel better doing it with your sister," Tigga suggested.

"I wanna do it. I'll call Kia and ask her if she still wants to go," Keller said excitedly.

"I guess we're going gun shopping tomorrow then," Tigga laughed as they continued to talk and eat.

"Yay!" Keller cheered.

"Yeah, I need something to relive my stress," Tigga said shaking his head.

"I'm sorry boo, but it's almost over," Keller smiled.

Since the first night they had sex in the hot tub in Florida, she and Tigga had been getting it in just about every day. She was on her cycle at the moment, so he had to wait it out. She gave him oral sex a few times, but that wasn't enough for him. Keller still thought that they were moving too fast, but she didn't know how to slow things down. Being with Tigga just felt right. It wasn't forced and the chemistry was undeniable. Things with them just flowed naturally and that was what Keller loved the most. Unfortunately, she had a feeling that the peace and quiet of their budding romance wouldn't last much longer. The uneasy feeling in the pit of her stomach just wouldn't go away. Once Anaya and Leo found out about them being together, it probably never would.

Chapter 24

"Rich, baby please answer the phone," Anaya begged for the fifth time in less than an hour.

She'd been calling him for two days straight and he hadn't answered any of her calls. They were supposed to spend a few days together since her girls were with Tigga, but Rich had been avoiding her. He wanted them to spend time at her house, but Anaya suggested that they get a room. She had just started working at their local Family Dollar, so she even offered to pay for it. Instead of being happy about their plans, Rich went off on her. One month of separation from Tigga had turned into two and nothing between her and Rich had changed. Anaya still wouldn't let him come to the house and he was done playing the same game with her. She thought for sure that he would have come around by now, but he was still ignoring her. Tigga had dropped the girls off home the night before and Rich was still nowhere to be found.

"Mama, can we have some ice cream?" Anaya's oldest daughter Tia asked when she walked into the living room.

"Okay baby," Anaya answered.

"She said okay," Tia yelled to her other sisters. She was about to run back into the other room before Anaya stopped her.

"Who was at your daddy's house when y'all were over there?" Anaya asked her daughter.

"Nobody," Tia replied just like always.

"He didn't have a lady friend over there or nothing," she continued to pry.

"No, but he talked on the phone with her," Tia said making her mother's heart skip a beat.

"With who? What's her name?"

"I don't know, but my daddy said that we're going to see her soon," Tia replied.

"Has she ever been there when y'all were there?" Anaya asked.

"No, but she got clothes and stuff in my daddy's closet. And my daddy let us use some of her soap that was in the bathroom," Tia revealed before she walked away.

Anaya was happy when she left because the tears fell as soon as she did. Her mother was right. Tigga broke up with her and moved out to be with somebody else. That hurt more than anything, especially after she did so much to try to keep him there. She did Rich dirty behind a nigga who didn't even give a fuck about her. She knew without a doubt that Tigga had loved her once before, but he seemed to have no feelings for her at all anymore. And if that wasn't bad enough, thoughts of Rich being with somebody else were starting to drive her crazy as well. Picking up her phone once again, Anaya decided to give her best friend Erica another call.

"That bastard still didn't answer the phone for you?" Erica asked when she picked up.

"Nope," Anaya sighed in defeat.

"His ass is right outside. I just told him that you were looking for him," Erica replied.

"And what did he say?" Anaya questioned.

"He didn't say anything. He just walked outside and started talking to his friends."

"That nigga must take me to play with. I'm about to put some clothes on and come over there. He can't ignore if I'm right up in his face," Anaya snapped in anger.

"Come on through girl. I'll be home," Erica said.

Anaya was about to reply until she heard her daughter's screaming in the other room.

"Mama! Something is wrong with Amari!" Tia yelled.

"She's shaking!" Talia screamed.

Anaya jumped up from the sofa and ran into the room with the phone still glued to her ear.

"Oh my God! Amari!" She yelled frantically when she saw her baby girl on the bedroom floor shaking violently.

"What's wrong Anaya?" Erica yelled.

"Send an ambulance to my house Erica. My baby is having a seizure," Anaya yelled.

Her other girls were crying hysterically as she led them out of the room and into the living room. Once Amari stopped shaking, Anaya laid her on her side just like she'd been instructed to do once before. She was able to breathe a little easier when Erica sent her a text telling her that an ambulance was in route to her house and so was she. She covered her baby girl up with a blanket and immediately dialed Tigga's number to let him know what was going on. When she got his voicemail three times in a row, she dialed Tessa'a number and prayed that she would answer.

***

"Are you mad?" Keller asked while looking across the table at Tigga.

They were out eating dinner at one of her favorite soul food restaurants when she hit him with some bullshit about getting her own apartment. Keller loved that she could talk to Tigga about anything without reservations. Unlike Leo, he asked her what she wanted to do instead of telling her what she was going to do. He valued her opinion and that meant a lot.

"Nah, I'm not mad, I'm pissed," Tigga replied.

"But why?" Keller asked like she didn't already know.

"You're not making sense to me right now Keller. Why would you go spend money to rent an apartment when I've offered to let you stay with me for as long as you want to?"

"I know Tigga, but I need to be settled. I have clothes at four different houses and that just don't make sense," Keller replied.

Aside from his house, Keller had belongings by Kia, Tessa, and Mo's houses. She divided her time up with all four of them, but she was with Tigga the most.

"That's your fault though Keller. My girls already know you. That was your decision to leave and go sleep somewhere else when they come over there. You think I give a fuck if they tell Anaya anything? She gon' find out sooner or later anyway. That shit don't make a bit of sense," Tigga argued.

"I didn't bring it up to start an argument. I just wanted to know how you felt about it," Keller replied.

"I don't want to argue with you either baby, but I don't agree with you getting your own apartment. You just told me not too long ago that you be scared and nervous when you're by yourself. Why would you want to get an apartment that you'll probably never sleep in?" Tigga questioned.

Keller looked away because she knew that he was right. She would probably be paying rent in a place that she would hardly ever sleep in. But she didn't want to smother Tigga by being in his space all the time either. He said that he loved her being around, but she wasn't so sure.

"Look at me Keller," Tigga said as he gently turned her head back around to face him. "Now tell me what's really going on?"

"You would tell me if you needed your space wouldn't you?" Keller questioned.

"You can't be serious right now," Tigga replied while grabbing her hand.

"You know how I am Tigga. I just have to be sure," Keller said.

"You need to stop with all the doubts Keller. I agree, we did move fast, but you can't put a timer on everything. It's not like we just met. We just decided to be in a relationship. I'm almost thirty years old and I don't have time for the games. I need to know right here, right now. Are you with me or not?" Tigga asked while looking her in her eyes.

"I'm with you baby." Keller said making him smile.

"Cool, so that means no more sleeping out when my girls come over. That's your house too and you don't have to ever leave it if you don't want to," Tigga replied.

"Okay," Keller smiled.

"Maybe now you can start claiming me as your man," Tigga teased her.

"I always claim you as my man," Keller replied right as his phone started ringing.

When Tigga looked at his phone and saw that it was Anaya, he declined her call and gave Keller his undivided attention once again. Anaya had been calling him all night and he didn't have time to be arguing with her.

"You can answer it baby," Keller said when the phone buzzed on the table a few seconds later.

"I'm good. I don't have time for Anaya and her bullshit. She's always calling for dumb shit just to piss me off. Her stupid ass called me for some washing liquid the other day," Tigga said making Keller laugh.

"Stop lying," Keller chuckled right as her phone started ringing, displaying Tessa's phone number. She answered with a huge smile on her face, but it disappeared when Tessa started talking.

"What's wrong?" Tigga asked when he saw Keller's facial expression.

"Okay Tessa, I'll tell him right now," Keller said right before she hung up the phone.

"What happened?" Tigga questioned.

"Tessa said that Amari just got rushed to the hospital. She had a seizure," Keller replied while giving him all the details that Tessa had just given her.

"Shit," Tigga yelled as he jumped up from the table.

He reached into his pocket and pulled out some money and threw it on the table. Keller grabbed her purse and was right behind him as he rushed out of the front door and headed to his car. They were about twenty minutes away from children's hospital, so Tigga wasted no time making his way over there. Keller could tell that he was nervous and she understood why. Tigga ran red lights and stop signs trying to get to his destination. Keller not only prayed for Amari's health, she also prayed for them to get there in one piece as well. She was happy when they finally pulled up to the hospital and parked in the visitor's parking lot.

"You want me to wait downstairs for you?" Keller asked once they walked through the front doors.

"No, come on," Tigga replied as he grabbed her hand and walked up to the nurse's station.

After getting Amari's room number, they got onto the elevator and made their way to her room. Amari's room was at the end of the hall, but Tigga could see a few people standing outside of the room as they walked in that direction. Donna was the first person to look his way and she was pissed when she saw Keller walking up with him. She remembered Keller's face from seeing them out at the restaurant not too long ago. Before Tigga could utter one word, Anaya stepped out of the room and rushed right over to him.

"What the fuck is this bitch doing here with you?" Anaya yelled while pointing to Keller.

"Where is my daughter?" Tigga asked while tightening his grip around Keller's waist.

"Don't worry about where she is. Answer my fucking question," Anaya yelled.

"Calm down Naya," one of her auntie's said as she walked over and rubbed her back.

"Fuck that! This bitch got me all the way fucked up right now. I knew something was up with y'all when we went to Florida," Anaya continued to yell.

"That's enough Anaya. Security is gonna throw all of us out here if you don't stop screaming," her mother yelled.

"I don't give a fuck! He's a disrespectful ass nigga for even bringing that hoe here."

Tigga wasn't in the mood to deal with Anaya's stupid ass at the moment, so he just ignored her. Keller didn't seem fazed by her ranting either, but that didn't stop her from going off. He was happy when he saw Tessa and his mother walking down the hall and he was sure that Keller was too.

"Bitch I know you knew about this too. You're probably the one who hooked them up," Anaya screamed at Tessa as soon as she and Christy walked up.

"How is Amari?" Tessa asked while ignoring Anaya. It wasn't the time for pettiness and it definitely wasn't the place.

"I don't even know. She's too busy acting a fool to tell me anything," Tigga answered.

"Where are the other girls?" Christy asked to no one in particular.

"Erica picked them up and took them home with her," one of Anaya's aunties spoke up.

"Y'all can leave. I don't want you here to see my baby with that bitch. I'm calling security," Anaya yelled.

"What's going on with Amari?" Christy asked.

"I don't know nothing ma. I just got here too," Tigga replied in aggravation.

Anaya was serious about calling security and they assured her that they were on their way up. When the elevator down the hall chimed a few minutes later, she was happy when she saw two officers step out and head down the hall towards them.

"What's going on? Is there a problem?" One of the officers asked as soon as he walked up to them.

"No officer, everything is fine," Christy replied.

"Everything is not fine. I am the mother of the patient and I want them gone," Anaya said pointing at Tigga and Keller.

"Why are you doing this Anaya? You should be ashamed of yourself," Christy fussed.

"Fuck all that dumb shit! Where is my daughter? That's all that I'm concerned about right now," Tigga yelled angrily making people come out of their rooms to see what was going on.

"You need to calm down sir. This is a hospital and there are other patients on this floor. I can't have all of y'all standing in the hallway like this. I'll let the parents and the grandparent's stay. Everybody else needs to go to the waiting room," the officer informed them.

Anaya was heated when she saw Tigga whispering something in Keller's ear. She almost lost it when he bent down and kissed Keller on the lips right before she and Tessa walked away. Anaya's aunts and cousin followed behind them, but they bypassed the waiting room and went outside instead. That left Tigga and Christy alone with Anaya and her mother. Security hung around jut to make sure everybody stayed calm.

"Can I see my daughter now?" Tigga asked calmly right as the elevator down the hall chimed once again.

"Awe shit," Donna mumbled loud enough for everyone to hear.

Everyone looked in the direction of the man and woman who were walking towards them, but not everyone knew who they were. Anaya's heart started beating fast and her palms were sweating like crazy when she saw Rich and his mother walking in their direction. As bad as she wanted to see him earlier, she wished he would just disappear right now. Talking to Tigga about anything was out of the question at the moment. She was heartbroken when she saw him walk up with Keller, but she still wasn't ready for him to find out about Rich.

"Rich, let me talk to you for a minute," Donna said trying to lead her daughter's past mistake back down the hall.

"Nah, we don't have nothing to talk about. What's up Anaya?" He said while looking over at her.

"Nothing is up," Anaya replied in almost a whisper.

"So you've been trying to call me day about nothing?" Rich questioned with a scowl on his face.

He knew without a doubt who Tigga was, but he didn't know by looking at his pictures that he was so tall and buffed. Rich was pretty tall himself, but he was damn near looking up to Tigga. The nigga's look screamed money which made Rich even more intimidated by him. Just by looking at him he could see why Anaya chose Tigga over him. He was fooling himself thinking that he could compete with the other man and he was done trying. He knew that the other woman standing there with him was his mother because Anaya had pointed her out to him on several occasions.

"We'll talk later Rich. This is not a good time," Anaya mumbled nervously.

"Y'all can do this on your own time. I need to go see about Amari," Tigga said as he and Christy walked over to the hospital room door.

"This is not the time or the place Rich. Just leave and let Anaya call you later," Donna suggested.

"I'm not going nowhere," Rich yelled in anger.

"Keep it down sir," one of the security guards warned. "Now y'all can either leave or go sit in the waiting room down hall. Only the parents and grandparents are allowed back here right now."

"Cool, then we're in the right place," Rich replied making Anaya cringe.

"And what is that supposed to mean?" Christy questioned him with her hands on her hips.

"It means that you and your son can leave. Amari is my daughter and her granddaughter," Rich replied smugly while pointing to his mother.

Stay tuned. Part two is coming soon...

51439852R00091

Made in the USA
San Bernardino, CA
01 September 2019